Delete Code

A Thriller

Book Seven in the Purple Frog Series

Harry F. Bunn

First published in 2022

All rights reserved. No part of this publication may be reproduced, stored in, or included in a retrievable system or transmitted in any form, or by any means, without the permission of the author.

Copyright © 2022 by LifeMadeSimple, LLC

DISCLAIMER

Delete Code is a work of fiction. Although much of the backdrop and the locations are real, most of the companies cited and all of the characters are fictitious and purely conjured up by the mind of the author.

Editing by J.H. Fleming

Formatting by Marissa Lete

Cover design by Daniel Eyenegho

ISBN 9798840743669

This book is dedicated to Beryl Ball, my late mother-in-law. A wonderful and much-loved lady!

Rest in peace.

Table of Contents

Chapter One 1

Chapter Two 11

Chapter Three 18

Chapter Four 25

Chapter Five 33

Chapter Six 44

Chapter Seven 53

Chapter Eight 62

Chapter Nine 72

Chapter Ten 81

Chapter Eleven 89

Chapter Twelve 96

Chapter Thirteen 109

Chapter Fourteen 118

Chapter Fifteen 129

Chapter Sixteen 134

Chapter Seventeen 144

Chapter Eighteen 151

Chapter Nineteen 157

Chapter Twenty 165

Chapter Twenty-One 172

Chapter Twenty-Two 183

Chapter Twenty-Three.. 190
Chapter Twenty-Four 198
Chapter Twenty-Five.. 205
Chapter Twenty-Six... 215
Chapter Twenty-Seven 227
Chapter Twenty-Eight.. 243
Chapter Twenty-Nine 251
Chapter Thirty 259
Chapter Thirty-One... 266
Chapter Thirty-Two... 274
Chapter Thirty-Three.. 286
About the Author: 299

Chapter One

Mike's computer screen suddenly went blank. A minute before, it had displayed a popular application, but now, nothing.

"Yes!" Mike Young, a programmer, looked at the dark screen and tried, without success, to restore the application. He attempted to reach other applications or files on the computer, but found none. He performed several sequences and verified that the computer had lost all of its data, programs, and operating system. Checking the cloud backup for these files showed him that they, too, had been erased. Ordinarily, this would have been a mystery and an incredible problem, but Young smiled. This was exactly what he had hoped for.

He turned to his main computer, which showed a few lines of code. It was this code that Mike had downloaded to his new system and then triggered to erase the data. Months before, as he'd developed the program, Young had decided to call it the "delete code," and he was elated at the belief that what he had developed provided him a path to unlimited riches. What company or government wouldn't pay him ransom money when faced with the options of doing so or losing all their data and software?

The code had taken him only a few months to write, which for a few lines seemed excessive, but it had been written and fine-tuned for functionality and brevity. It did not perform a complex routine, but embraced an art form of simplicity. The code looked benign as well, which would help prevent its detection.

He scoured the program for errors he might have made, but found none. His mind cycled through the various situations which might arise and how the code would handle each. He nodded. Everything was covered.

The next stage in his plan would be more difficult. He needed to upload the code to the computers he would target, but not knowing which these would be, he decided on a broader approach. He would upload his code to every personal computer and server on the planet.

This was not a trivial task, and would require a vehicle that would spread the malware across the two billion computers currently installed.

Even ten years before, most software upgrades were installed when the user requested them. Now, most software was upgraded automatically. The software provider decided when an upgrade would be released and sent the new code over the internet to every computer using that application. To distribute his delete code, he needed to hack into a ubiquitous software upgrade from a major software provider that had near-universal coverage and piggyback his malware on it.

Logically, the software company would be Microsoft, Apple, or Google, since software from those vendors was universally used, but each of those vendors used anti-hacking protections that were too great for even his ability. He needed another approach, so he searched the dark web for malware secrets and discovered a small software company, Realizmm, that provided a few simple widgets that were incorporated into most of the browser software available. One allowed characters to appear with highlights when selected. A simple function, but fundamental, and most software vendors incorporated the widget rather than writing their own code. If he could add his code to the upgrade, the next time the widget was updated, his code would be installed worldwide--not perfectly, but probably on eighty to ninety percent of installed personal computers and servers. The software company, Realizmm, utilized solid firewalls and first-rate security, but not as great as the technology giants, so it was an easier target.

The next evening, he attempted his first intrusion into the Realizmm servers. It was not successful, and his effort triggered an alert which caused him to hastily exit his computer and sever its connection with the internet.

"Damn!"

He was frustrated, but an idea came to him. He spent some time thinking this through and then accessed a series of servers across the world. He would use these to simulate an attack from several thousand computers on the software company's website while shielding his identity.

"Classic denial of service attack," he said out loud as the idea struck him.

He implemented the strike the next day, and within the first hour, the huge traffic driven to their servers brought down Realizmm's systems. As their IT staff worked to bring their systems back online, they turned off their firewall for just one minute, but this was enough for Young's trojan program, which he had developed separately, to take advantage of the momentary drop in their defenses. His software infiltrated their network and established a backdoor to Realizmm's IT infrastructure.

Young terminated the attack and waited to ensure the company had not tracked him in any way. He did nothing for another week until he felt he was safe.

At the end of the week, he accessed the software backdoor and loaded his delete code into the latest version of the widget software. Now, the next upgrade to Realizmm's software that was sent to the browser companies for incorporation in their next update would carry his code with it. Worldwide distribution might take another week or more, but the proliferation of his malware was inevitable, unless the browser companies or the widget company discovered the rebel code and disabled it.

Various geek websites tracked software updates, and Mike found that the next upgrade from Realizmm would be released the following Monday.

"Shazam. Malware Monday."

Mike lived in an attic flat in a low-cost area of Bradford in the United Kingdom, and for several months he had written and fine-tuned his code. During that time, he had subsisted on canned meats and vegetables, plus a nightly treat of canned peaches in syrup. Normally Mike shaved each day, but for the past month, as the code neared completion, he had not done so. Nor had he bathed more than once a week. His hair was long, needed cutting, and was greasy.

He was out of beer, and looking at his computer screen, knew now was a time of waiting until the following Monday to see if his code had been discovered. If not, he would be able to test its functionality. Until then, there was nothing to do, so he decided to visit his local pub. He would meet a fellow programmer, a girl, who like him was in her early twenties. She had significant piercings and tattoos and had convinced Mike to have a large tattoo inked on his upper left arm. He resented the pain, the time it took, and the cost, and decided early that he didn't like the tattoo anyway. One of his first purchases, when he came into wealth, would be the tattoo's removal.

"Hi, Cate." He waved to her as she entered the pub in the northern British city and made her way through the crowd to the table where he sat.

"Beer?" she asked him.

———⁕———

"Yes." She was wearing torn jeans and a voluminous dark hoodie, but it did nothing to hide her large shape. Her jeans were naturally torn, rather than the fashionable ones purchased in an already torn state. She suspected that Mike did not find her particularly attractive, but believed that he respected her coding skills, and she had made a few thousand pounds in a recent ransomware attack. She had come close to being arrested when the scheme was tracked by the cybercrime squad in London, but had managed to elude the authorities.

The bartender pulled down on the lever of Newcastle Brown Ale and filled two pint glasses. She took a quick slurp from one and carried the two back to the table where Mike sat. She could tell he was excited about something.

"What have you been up to, Mike? I haven't seen you in months."

"I've just pulled off the hack of the century. Perhaps the hack of all time."

"Yeah, yeah." She teased him, although she knew he was not someone who boasted about things that he believed false.

"It's true. I now have within my grasp access to as much money as I could ever want. Billions of pounds."

"Sounds like you're back on coke again, Mike." She was skeptical and took a gulp of her beer.

"No. Really. This is the big score. The biggest."

"Did you hack into a bank?"

"Sort of."

"Sort of?"

"Actually, I have hacked into every bank. Worldwide. And every government and every company and every home."

Cate shook her head. "Shit. When do you get arrested?" She could not help appearing cynical.

"I won't."

"Okay, so what is this super hack?"

"Next Monday, my few, perfect lines of code will be installed on nearly every PC and server around the world, and I'll be able to access them. All computers at the same time. Or I can select one or more for attack. I can filter using a set of IP addresses to select the computers and activate my code just on those."

"Cool. So, what does your magic software do?"

"Not much. Just wipe out all data on the device."

Cate scoffed. "People have a backup. They'll just download from the cloud and start up again."

"My code traces the backup and deletes it as well. Think about it. I call MI6 and tell them that if they don't remit, I don't know, a billion pounds, I'll delete all their files worldwide, including their backups."

Cate let out a whistle.

"Does it work?"

"I think so, but Monday is the day it will be downloaded through a browser software update. I can test it then."

"Can you wipe out all the data for a country?" She thought she knew the answer, but had to ask.

"Yes. If Russia had my code, they could have taken over Ukraine at no cost, without any military losses, no civilian losses, no destruction of industry, and within less than half an hour."

"I guess, if you want to, you can delete all the data on the planet." Her eyes widened. "That would cause the greatest economic meltdown ever."

"Yes, it would. But I don't want power. What I want is money. Heaps and heaps of money." He returned to his beer, which had grown warm while he told his story.

While Mike Young had been scrupulous in his safeguards to avoid being discovered and identified online, he had not carried over this trait to his conversation with Cate. A man sitting alone at the table next to them removed an old notebook, and with the stub of a well-worn pencil, took down notes of the conversation he had just overheard. He was wearing an old but clean and freshly pressed pair of overalls with an embroidered name and title--Bob, Janitor.

Looking at his notes, his face spread into a smile as he thought of how much this information might be worth.

Chapter Two

As Mike drank his second beer, he became aware of how unwise it was to be talking about the delete code in public.

"This is probably not the place to be discussing this. Let's buy some beers and go back to my place. We can talk more freely there."

"You just want to get into my pants, don't you, Mike?"

"Maybe later, but let's go back and drink the beers first."

He could tell she was anxious to hear more about his code and how he planned to use it, so she nodded her agreement, and since she'd made a significant amount of cash from her last ransomware gig, he allowed her to pay for the dozen bottles of lager.

When they were alone back at his flat, he elaborated on how his malware would be downloaded.

"Okay, so you've downloaded the code to every computer on the planet. What next?"

"Next, I test it."

"Okay, let's say the code works. What next?"

"I'll target some company and threaten to delete all their files unless they pay me."

"Which company?"

"I haven't thought through the specifics, but I'll probably start with a bank, maybe in a foreign country."

"Which country?"

"Don't know yet, but one where they'll hide the fact that they've been hacked so they don't upset their customers. I don't want the whole world alerted and the cops to start chasing me from the start."

"Sounds good."

She glanced around as if seeking inspiration for her next question.

"How do you trigger the code?"

Mike was still basking in the fact that Cate, someone he admired for her coding abilities, had already expressed genuine praise for his creation. But he was also aware that she was grilling him about details that he might want to keep to himself. He trusted her, but she was, after all, a thief, and with the huge gains at stake, she might be able to rationalize taking advantage of him.

"That's my little secret."

They talked more and drank more until Mike, who had not been drinking while he wrote the code, realized that he was drunk.

"I think I'm smashed."

"Yes, you are. Let's stop now and you can take me to bed. I don't have the energy to walk home tonight, so you can stick your thing in me."

The next day, Mike woke early and gazed across his bed to the heavily snoring Cate. He left the bed and padded barefoot to his small kitchen and opened the refrigerator. It contained the mandatory open box of baking soda and he glanced at the date that the product's manufacturer recommended the powder be replaced. It was three years before, just a year after he had moved into his flat. Other than the baking soda, the fridge was empty. His eyes traversed his living room, which was next to the kitchen, and he saw the dozen empty beer bottles scattered around. He decided he would clear up the mess later.

He owned a small espresso machine and filled its water reservoir with water from the tap before adding the coffee and turning the device on. A light glowed red, and he knew it would be a few minutes before it turned to green, indicating the water was heated and ready to brew the coffee.

He looked over at Cate. She was a brilliant programmer, and she'd seemed truly impressed when he'd told her about his delete code.

He thought back to the previous night. Their sex had been reasonable, but in his inebriated state, he had not been on his best form, and he could not remember much about it. The light on the espresso machine clicked to green and awoke Mike from his reverie.

A week later, on what he called Malware Monday, Mike ensured that most of his own computers had the automatic update feature disabled so the new software containing the delete code did not install on them. He left one unguarded. As he sat in front of his main screen, he remembered that he had not mentioned this to Cate and wondered if she had thought to also shield herself from the code. He laughed. *Perhaps I can blackmail her as well.* He looked at his calendar and verified that the malware should have been distributed worldwide by then. Now the moment of truth. Had Realizmm or the browser companies detected the code's presence and disabled it? If not, was the code distributed as he'd expected? If it was now installed worldwide, would he be able to destroy individual groups of computers from his dashboard, which controlled access to the remote systems?

A sudden thought hit him. What if his code was flawed and on installation triggered the delete function? Had he just destroyed every computer and database on planet earth?

He checked the one computer which should have been upgraded with the delete code and was pleased to see that the malware was in place but had not been triggered.

Mike did not have a large family, but there was one cousin, about his age, in Australia, and he emailed him requesting a chat by phone. From the email reply, he used another software app to locate the IP address of his cousin's WiFi router. Mike keyed this into the dashboard he had created for the delete code and called his cousin's phone.

"G'day," his cousin said as he took the call.

"Hi. It's Mike. Long time."

"Yeah, Mike. I guess you want something from me. You only ever call when you need help." The phone went quiet for a minute and then his cousin continued.

"If it's money you want, forget it. You haven't paid me back the two hundred dollars you sponged off me last time. I'm not stupid."

Mike did not like his cousin, nor the interchange of their conversation. Perhaps he was being harsh. Australians had a tendency of being direct in their conversations compared with the British, who had a tendency to deliver messages so subtle that the recipient was often unaware of what they were being told. He decided to match his cousin's direct approach.

"Listen, Bas. It's not like that. I just want to show you something on a website that I thought might be of interest."

"Okay, but this had better not be a scam."

Mike dictated a web address and waited to make sure that his cousin had his computer turned on. He heard him starting to key in the web address. The site was random, and its contents meant nothing, but Mike would use this ploy to ensure that this one individual, on the far side of the earth, had his computer active and was intently looking at his screen. Mike had previously entered the IP address of his cousin's router to his dashboard, and clicked an icon marked "Delete." He waited for his cousin's reaction.

"Shit, Mike. My screen just went blank. Bloody Microsoft. But no problem, I'll reboot."

Mike waited, smiling broadly.

"This is weird. I can't access anything on my computer. Don't know what's going on."

"Not to worry, Bas. Not that important anyway, but I'll send you the website URL and you can look it up when you get your computer going again." Mike knew his cousin's computer was fried and he would never be able to restart it. He gazed at his watch and the time in Sydney. "Have a great morning, Bas!"

He sat back in his ergonomically designed office chair and inspected his dashboard.

He said out loud, "It worked. It fucking worked."

Chapter Three

Purple Frog was the brainchild of a billionaire, Jason Overly, and he had monitored its activities over its eight years in operation. His choice as director, Silvia Lewis, had built a strong team of analysts, profilers, and translators, as well as specialist groups in money laundering, hacking, and field operations. Initially, he had intended to provide only oversight to the organization and have little to do with its often illegal operations. His responsibilities as CEO of his technology company, Avanch, gave him little time for other activities.

But as time passed, he established succession plans for Avanch and built a strong team that was able to operate largely independent of his skills. He became less involved in the technology company and more involved with Purple Frog, finding the excitement, risk, and sometimes danger of the clandestine spy agency dedicated to fostering world peace, a welcome relief from the corporate world. His days now at Avanch were driven by internal politics,

Wall Street challenges, competition, government regulation, activist investors, and the media. Recently, he had realized that he was sick of the day-to-day job of running a major company.

Then Sarah, his wife of thirty years, had shown signs of poor health. She experienced unexpected weight loss, shortness of breath, and excessive night sweats. Their family doctor had ordered several tests, and after consulting with a specialist, the diagnosis was that she was suffering from a rare blood cancer. This had reached an advanced stage and the specialist had informed Sarah and Jason that her condition was terminal. They'd sought other opinions, but the prognosis each time was similar.

"How long?" Jason had asked.

"Hard to say. Maybe six months, maybe eight."

Sarah accepted the verdict, but Jason was devastated and reached out to other medical specialists and professionals for a way to cure her ailment, or at least to treat it.

They tried all the standard approaches, visiting five specialists across the U.S. When none of these could offer hope beyond standard treatments, which would provide minimal added longevity and make her remaining time uncomfortable, they turned to some experimental treatments. When these failed too, Jason discovered a clinic in Switzerland that offered a possible alternative and they flew to Geneva to consult the doctors there. This treatment also failed to stop the spread of the cancerous cells.

"I've wanted to come to Geneva for years..." Sarah said before falling asleep in his arms on the flight back to their home in California.

While some doctors suggested that there was a small chance that she might beat the cancer, as each new treatment was shown to be ineffective, Jason started to accept that within the next few months he would lose the woman he had loved since the day they first met at a football game at Princeton University.

Sarah slept a lot of the time as the cancer cells multiplied in her body and the painkilling drugs fought to keep her comfortable.

One morning, she reached over the bed to him and said, "Darling, we both know nothing is working, so let's go down to St. Croix to Sugar Ridge and at least I can die in a place I love."

"But the medical facilities are limited there."

"They're not going to cure me here, so why does it matter?"

"I guess I can have a specialist fly down with us and stay on..." He did not complete the sentence.

"That would be nice." She dozed off and Jason shook, holding back tears he had hidden since the first day he'd heard her fatal diagnosis.

The next evening, Jason attended an Avanch board meeting at the company's headquarters in Cupertino. A senior director--who had been a friend of Jason's for many years, as well as a long-term member of the board--asked the question all the members wanted to have answered. "How is Sarah doing?"

"Not good. The consensus is that she has only a month or two left."

The senior director twisted uneasily in his chair and then said, "It's not just Sarah who's suffering, Jason. Over the last few months, Avanch has faced a lot of headwinds, and you haven't been around to make the decisions that needed to be made. Anil has done very well, but he's been hesitant to make major decisions without your approval. We understand and sympathize with your need to look after Sarah, but we have an obligation to the shareholders to ensure the health and success of Avanch."

Jason had been looking at the blank yellow pad he had brought into the meeting and had only half listened to what had just been said. Then his mind clicked into place.

"What are you saying? You know Sarah has to take precedence."

"That's the problem, Jason. Perhaps you need to take some time off. Perhaps hand over the reins to Anil." The director knew Anil well and he was the logical successor to Jason.

"Are you bastards firing me?" Jason was furious, an emotion he rarely displayed.

The senior director had known him for over ten years and was embarrassed, but Jason's temper had been triggered. Jason now stood, shaking his fist at all the board members.

"Get out, all of you. You're fired. I never want to see any of you again, and you can forget stock options at the end of the year." They knew he could not carry through on his demand for their resignations and they stood their ground.

"Jason..."

Overly strode to the door, opened it, and left the boardroom. He returned to his office a little way down the corridor and flung himself into an armchair, shaking with rage coupled with a feeling of remorse for his childish actions.

There was a knock on his door. "Come in."

The senior director entered Overly's office and Jason motioned him to be seated.

"Jason, I'm sorry. I handled that badly and you were right to be mad at all of us."

"I get it, but you're right. I've thought about making the move for a while now, even before Sarah became ill. It was just a shock. When it comes to decisions like this, it's always been me that made them, not others."

His friend walked over to a small credenza and pulled out a bottle of Henry McKenna Single Barrel bourbon and two glasses.

"It's after six, so let's have a drink."

"Sorry. I should have offered." The wind had gone from Overly's sails, and he slumped down, slurping the whiskey his friend had poured.

Overly nodded.

"Anil has been an excellent Chief Operating Officer, and is ready to take the reins as Chief Executive. I'll talk to him about it tomorrow. All the board members know him well, so it should be straightforward. I'll be available to help in any way I can. I obviously want Avanch to succeed. It makes sense, since I still own nearly four percent of the stock."

Two days later, Overly and Sarah, accompanied by a medical specialist, were driven to the San Francisco airport, boarded Jason's private jet, and flew down to their home in St. Croix, where Sarah would spend her remaining weeks.

Chapter Four

Bob, the man who had overheard the conversation between Mike and Cate in the Bradford pub, had not had a very successful life. After leaving high school with poor grades, neither he nor his parents had even considered higher education. He had worked in a janitorial role at several office buildings and earned a paltry living. However, he did enjoy a strong and outgoing personality, and was able to converse easily with everyone he encountered. These included his current bosses in the largest conglomerate in the area, Ayling Industries.

Ayling had been founded as a textile company over a century before, but the current managing director's father had seen the woolen material industry being destroyed by cheaper products from other countries and had shifted focus to engineering, packaging, and chemicals. However, it now faced headwinds from Britain's withdrawal from the EU and the rapid expansion of higher-quality products from China and India. The British business press had picked up problems at the company, and with a play on the company name, described Ayling Industries as "ailing."

Jeff Ayling sat at his large desk, looking at a thick printed report. It was the only paper on the desk, and on the right of the polished wood surface he had two trays--an "in tray" and an "out tray", and each had just one or two documents in it. His current attention was focused on the hefty report that he had before him. It had been written by the company's accounting firm and raised the likelihood of bankruptcy for the privately held organization. The report recommended that Ayling review the details contained in a spreadsheet that had been sent to him by email. Ayling knew this could be accessed from his desktop personal computer, which one of his technical people had installed for him several years before. It sat in the corner of his office. Ayling had never used it. *It's all right for techies and kids, but give me paper every time.*

There was a knock on his door, and he called out, "Come in."

His secretary, who preferred to be called by the modern term "personal assistant," entered his sprawling office on the top floor of the company's headquarters in a fashionable part of the northern city.

"Sorry to bother you, Mr. Ayling, but the janitor, Bob, says he has something urgent to tell you about."

Ayling was annoyed by the interruption.

"Crap. He's probably found a rat in the basement. I don't have time for this. Have him tell you what he wants and you can pass it on if it's important."

"I tried that, but he was insistent."

Ayling liked Bob and enjoyed a hearty repartee with him on the infrequent times when they met.

"Bloody man. All right, ask him to come in." *At least it's something less stressful than the damn accountants' report.*

The janitor was wearing brown overalls, but they were clean and pressed and his hair had been washed. This was true to character for Bob, whom Ayling regarded as a proud working-class man. He wondered what the janitor wanted to talk about.

"Morning, Bob. How have you been? And how is Mabel doing?" One of Ayling's skills was an encyclopedic memory for the names of the spouses and families of many of his workers.

"We're all doing fine, Mr. Ayling. Thank you, sir."

"So, what can I do for you?"

The janitor shuffled from foot to foot, giving the appearance of being unsure of what to do next.

"You see, sir, rumor has it that the company's suffering a rough patch at the moment, and I may be able to help."

"That's poppycock. Ayling Industries is doing just fine." He was aware that the janitor did not believe a word he had just spoken.

"Well, sir, let me tell you about a conversation I happened to overhear down at the pub the other night."

When Bob left his office, Jeff Ayling walked to a comfortable leather armchair and dropped his large body into it. The story Bob had told him was unbelievable. Ayling had learned a reasonable amount about cyberattacks from discussions with his IT manager and the accounting firm which audited his accounts. He knew he should pass on the information that Bob had relayed to the local police, or perhaps Scotland Yard in London. But he paused. If he could find a way to work with the hacker, even in a small way, the cash flow issues Ayling Industries was facing might be able to be resolved.

He had not smoked for some years and had a rigorous policy in place at the company which prohibited smoking of any kind. But today was different. He was already thinking of breaking rules, probably breaking the law, and his desire for a cigarette was trivial by comparison. He arose and went to his desk drawer and removed an unopened pack of John Player Specials, a box of matches, and a small ashtray.

He sat down again and lit up as he thought about various options. *Blackmail the hacker? Partner with the hacker?*

As he inhaled and then blew smoke out into the room, he made up his mind. He would do whatever was needed to benefit from what his janitor had found out. This would not be some small police reward. It would be bigger. Much bigger.

He knew this probably meant committing an illegal act, but he was sure that he was smart enough to evade capture. The police officers he had met over the years were not a very bright lot.

Rewarding Bob in some way would keep him silent, and Ayling decided he could not involve anyone else in the plan he was starting to formulate.

He stood, walked to his desk, and used his rather antiquated intercom to communicate with his secretary. "Jane, get Bob back up here now and block off my calendar for the next hour."

The British hacker, Mike Young, was ready for his first excursion into crime. His years of hacking until now had been little more than fun ego trips. There had been eleven of these, and he had proven his ability to outwit the checks and balances used to deter hackers. He had penetrated companies as a hobby, and none of these had provided any monetary reward. He had never thought through in advance how he could exploit his hack for gain.

The delete code would change this, and he decided that his first goal would be a demand for one million euros and his target would be a bank. He would launch an attack on a small bank somewhere outside the U.K.

He used the internet to research potential prey and came across a suitable target. Looking into the ownership of the bank, he failed to unearth much. The recorded owners were a series of companies, but each seemed to be headquartered in some foreign country. Accessing their website, he found little more information, and it was obvious that the bank kept a low profile.

However, the bank appeared to have significant reserves and would be easily able to comply with his demand. He reasoned that it would pay up and keep the theft secret rather than make it public and probably lose many or all of its customers.

Then he thought about a more practical matter. How would he collect the money? He envisioned a suitcase full of cash, but dismissed that as impractical. Twenty thousand, fifty-euro notes? Ten thousand one-hundred-euro notes? And even if he did collect the funds in cash, how could he hide it where it would be safe and away from the authorities' prying eyes? And how would he spend it? If he wanted to buy a Ferrari, he could not enter a car showroom and pay with cash without having to explain why he was not using a check or a wire transfer.

Maybe I'll get them to send the ransom as a wire transfer. They could send it to a foreign bank account. He knew little about offshore accounts other than what he'd read in the news, so he Googled the keyword phrases "money laundering" and "offshore banking." Half an hour later, he concluded that this was a sophisticated area and one where his lack of expertise could easily result in his apprehension by the police or the loss of the money to some dishonest bank or law firm. If the latter happened, he would take delight in using his delete code to destroy them, but that would not get his money back.

He cursed himself. *Why didn't I think about this before?* He had concentrated on the code, which was what he enjoyed and did best, but not the practicalities of dealing with the outcome. His thoughts went to a joke Cate had once told him about a dog chasing a bus with the punch line being, *"But what will the dog do with the bus if the dog catches it?"*

He was also facing a personal cash flow issue. He had not held a paying job for six months and had just purchased a new laptop and destroyed it to test his code. He was behind on his rent, and though he had few expenses, he was running desperately short of cash. He held his head in his hands and then his phone rang.

"Is this Mike Young?"

"Yes. Who's calling?"

"My name is Bob, and I'd like to meet with you."

"How did you get my number?"

"It was quite difficult, but perseverance pays off, mate."

"Are you selling something?"

"No. I want to meet, and if our little talk goes well, I have a man who wants to work with you. Something like a partnership."

"I don't understand."

"We know you're a hacker, and we want to talk, mate."

"Shit."

Chapter Five

Ching Tong sat at his desk and thought about his work at Purple Frog. He had joined the clandestine organization in its early days and worked closely with its various departments.

He was aware that all sixty of his colleagues regarded him as an arrogant son-of-a-bitch, but, rather than seeing this as disparaging, he took it as a badge of honor and reveled in what his colleagues saw as his egotism. He reasoned that they all acknowledged he was the best hacker on the planet and believed he had proven this many times over. His recent promotion to team leader in the hacker group had gone to his head, and he bounced up and down on his office chair as his fingers sped over the keys of the computer in front of him.

As it was his stock in trade, Ching spent many hours each day on the dark web exploring the rants and the boasts of hackers across the world as they bragged about their secrets to gain the appreciation of their peers. This foible brought many of them to the attention of the various government cyber sleuths, and many had been arrested over the years. Most regarded hacking as a game in which they competed with one another to commit bigger and better hacks. Their goal was to win against their fellows, similar to people competing in the wide range of video games online. Ching had a similar need for praise, but had to be content with receiving it only from his fellow froggies and Purple Frog management. Alan Harlan, his boss, had made it clear from the start that he was to keep a very low profile. Alan's boss, Silvia Lewis, also made this clear when she agreed to his promotion to team leader of the hacker group.

On this day, he picked up on a thread of communications in which one hacker expressed doubts that malware could be embedded in a legitimate software upgrade and distributed by piggybacking on this. The hacker pointed out the stringent checks that software providers made and declared this approach was currently impossible. Ching smiled. *Should I take this as a challenge?*

Then a new thread appeared from a hacker with the username of BigCat49. *Where do these people get their usernames?* thought Ching.

The thread was brief: "This is not impossible, and it's being done right now."

The thread took Ching's attention. He entered the chat stream with his current codename "78561KKII" and typed, "Tell me more."

There was a pause, and the earlier thread from BigCat49 disappeared. Whoever had commented had decided it was a mistake and he, or she, wanted to remove any evidence of the exchange. Ching had been unwilling to take the interchange seriously, but its immediate removal probably meant the claim was real and not an idle comment. He took note of the date and time and the name BigCat49. He would raise the issue at next Monday's meeting.

Bob met with Mike Young in the hacker's flat in Bradford in the late afternoon. Bob, who prided himself on neatness and a clean environment, looked around and shook his head as he entered. Mike seemed to have cleaned up to a limited extent, but to Bob, the place was dirty and disorganized, and he wondered whether this man was indeed an incredible hacker or whether this was all BS.

"Beer?" the hacker offered.

"No. Maybe after we've talked."

Mike attempted to take the initiative.

"I don't know what you were talking about on the phone because I'm not a hacker."

"Then why did you agree to meet?"

Mike paused. "I thought it would be fun." His hesitancy and nervousness showed clearly that this was not the case.

"Tell me, Mike. Do you mind if I call you Mike?"

"Mike is fine."

"So, tell me. What is this software thing you have created?" He motioned to the bank of computers that adorned Mike's kitchen table and at the expensive, ergonomic desk chair.

"It's my job," Mike said with a secret wish that he had paying employment at the moment. He continued, "I write software, and I am very good at it."

"How good?"

"The best."

Bob looked at the mass of intricate code which was displayed on the various computer screens. He could not understand any of it, but he decided there was probably value in what this programmer had to offer.

"Let's stop the pretense--I know you have some special code. I think it's called malware, which you have implanted on every computer on the planet."

"And if I did?"

"Doesn't sound legal to me, mate. I don't want to have to go to the police, but if we can't reach an agreement, that's just what I'll do."

Mike walked to the refrigerator and took out a cold beer. Bob observed there were only two beers in the refrigerator, and they were of the cheapest brand. Popping the top, Mike took a long gulp. "Do you want money? I don't have any."

"No. I want to talk about the possibility of a partnership. Actually, it's my boss who wants that, and any arrangement will be between you and him. I'm just a middleman."

"So, what does he want?"

Bob did not answer the question. "I'll include him in the next meeting and you two can thrash that out. He thinks he can help you. He's a smart man and knows the business world." He looked around at the peeling wallpaper on the walls of the kitchen area. "He can help with doing some sophisticated things. Better schemes, maybe funding the operation, laundering the proceeds..."

The last comment seemed to capture Mike's attention. "He understands money laundering?"

"Possibly."

"That might be interesting."

Bob realized he had stumbled on a pressure point that might make the partnership work. He didn't have a clue about hacking or malware or money laundering, but Jeff Ayling probably did. He decided to get out of the flat as quickly as possible and introduce his boss to the hacker and let them cut whatever deal made sense.

Looking around the squalid flat, Bob picked up on a metal whiteboard with writing on it made with a black erasable. He saw at the top "delete code" with a number of points laid out under it, which he took to be aspects of the code. All had been checked off, but at the bottom was a new subject: "game."

"So, you call it delete code, eh?"

"Yes. That's right."

Ayling had laid out two simple and clear objectives for Bob in this first meeting--verify that the code was probably real and decide what made the hacker tick. Bob now knew these answers.

After Bob left him, Mike slammed his head against the wall. He looked at his whiteboard. *Why the fuck didn't I erase that?*

This wasn't the way it was supposed to be. Before he had even embarked on his first heist, someone was muscling in and wanting a cut. He went to the refrigerator and took out a beer. It was his last.

He slumped down into his one armchair and thought about his situation. Though frustrating, if this mystery man could provide a mechanism for receiving the funds from his ransomware attacks and hiding them, the partnership might make sense. It was an area that had kept Mike awake at night since he'd realized it was fundamental. The idea of Bob's boss providing some interim funds would also be attractive.

He sat back and took a gulp of beer from the bottle in his hand. He reflected that the code was now installed on computers worldwide, and his power came from being able to activate its simple function. Sitting down behind his main computer, a high-end laptop, he accessed an entry screen. He entered a passcode and was prompted for another. Several steps later, his computer revealed a dashboard which was a more advanced version of the one he had used with his Australian cousin. The functions now enabled access to various programs which would seek and report IP addresses and computer identifiers, which would enable Mike to access one or a group of computers. After selecting those he wished to "delete," he would click on the large button at the bottom of his screen, which was labeled "Delete." With the levels of security protocol he had implemented to reach the dashboard, only he could trigger activation of the code. This ensured that he had final control.

A year previously, he had set up the whiteboard on the wall of his living room and often used it to order his thoughts. He now walked to it and was about to erase the whole set of text. Then he stopped. *Too bloody late, idiot*, he chastised himself. He regarded the one item that was unchecked, "game," which was to be his next endeavor, a video game he had envisioned as a hobby exercise, and sighed. *I may be an ace programmer, but...*

Later that day, Bob met with his boss. Ayling sat in his favorite armchair while the janitor stood.

"Mr. Ayling, the hacker is Mike Young, and I'm pretty certain he has the code and it's real."

"Good. Did you pick up anything that we can offer him other than not shopping him to the police?"

Bob took a long breath. "He likes being praised, but doesn't like being threatened. I threw out a few ideas and he latched onto money laundering as something of interest. I don't even know what laundering is, but he seemed to think it's important, and he doesn't seem to have a way to do it."

Ayling sat back while Bob remained standing. Ayling now smoked openly and blew smoke towards the janitor.

"Makes sense. He's a hacker. Just a crooked programmer, and he can blackmail people or companies with what his special code can do to them. But he needs a way to get paid, and to hide the payment from the police and the taxman."

It was 6:00 p.m. and Ayling walked over to a bar in the corner of his office next to his unused personal computer and poured himself a Scotch. "Drink, Bob?"

"That would be nice, sir."

"What's your poison?"

"Scotch looks good, sir."

After pouring his own, Ayling replaced the cork stopper in a bottle of an expensive single malt Scotch and Bob saw him reach for a less expensive, blended variety. He half-filled a tumbler for Bob and asked, "Ice?"

"That would be lovely."

Bob suspected Ayling knew little about laundering funds, but he might be able to convince the naïve hacker that he did. And he probably had contacts and they would do the laundering or whatever.

"Shall I set up a meeting, sir?"

"Yes. Tomorrow night, but I don't want to be seen going to his flat. I'll ask Jane to rent a room at that new hotel on the ring road and we can meet there."

Mike was a little scared. He had always been easily intimidated by people he accepted as his superiors, and this meeting was going to be stressful. One aspect which worried him was that he might cave in and give away too much of the proceeds from the heists.

He thought more about it. If the mystery man provided a sound mechanism to accept the extortion amounts, clean them, and make the funds available to him, it would be worth, say, ten percent of the first "transaction." This would provide nine hundred thousand euros for Mike and one hundred thousand euros for Mr. Mystery, as he now decided to refer to the man. Mike could get the whole one million by asking the target bank for about 1.11 million if he decided to, and this was just the start. When he later demanded billions, there would always be enough, and his Mr. Mystery would be more than satisfied. If Mr. Mystery was prepared to provide short term cash, it would be more than welcome. He had run out of beer and did not have the money to buy more. He was also down to only three cans of peaches.

His phone rang; it was 9:00 p.m.

"Hello, Mike. Tomorrow night, ten p.m. at the new Astor Hotel on the ring road. I'll let you know the room later. Okay?"

"Okay, Bob."

Chapter Six

The next evening, an Uber drove up to the hotel and Mike Young alighted. He had paid the rideshare on a credit card and knew he would not be able to clear the balance that month. As he stood in the car park, he wondered when he would receive details of which room he was to go to for the meeting. It was cold and raining lightly, and he was nervous and a little angry. He was being played by Bob and some other mystery individual whom he would meet this night.

His smartphone rang and he answered immediately. "This is Mike."

"Room two oh five." The caller hung up.

A few minutes later, the hacker looked across the bedroom at a large man sitting in the one chair in the room. He was wearing a mask reminiscent of the earlier COVID lockdowns and a hat. It was clear that these devices were there to safeguard the man's identity, and Mike almost laughed at the theatrical scene in front of him. Then his fears of this man stealing his amazing code or sabotaging it in some way returned. He sat on the bed closest to the window.

"Okay. I'm here. What do you want?"

There was no casual conversation about the weather or family or anything else. Mr. Mystery went straight to business.

"Mr. Young, my man here," he motioned to Bob, "has told me you have developed some very interesting software which has incredible potential. If this became known to the police, you wouldn't be able to make any money from your innovation and might well end up in jail. I want to keep your secret and allow you to exploit it."

Mike nodded slowly. This was what he'd expected. This man, whoever he was, wanted a piece of the action for keeping quiet. Mike's mind strayed to a movie he had seen many years before when someone had faced a similar problem and had resolved the issue by killing the blackmailer. However, Mike did not have a weapon and did not see himself as a killer.

The man said, "Before we talk further, may I ask you to tell me what this code is, what it does, and how you plan to make money from it?" The man signaled to Bob, who came forward with two glasses, a bottle of single malt Scotch, and a small bowl with ice cubes. He poured a drink for his boss and for the hacker and settled down on the second bed in the room.

"Cheers, Mike." The man raised his mask a little and took a sip.

Mike found the bed on which he was sitting rather uncomfortable, but did not see any option than to remain seated. He drank the Scotch, not really enjoying the sharp taste, and decided that beer was better. He had played through his options over and over again in the lead-up to the meeting, and finally concluded that he would tell the man about his achievements and see where that led. He had decided the smart strategy was to downplay the code's capability, but now concluded that his potential partner was intelligent and would see through the ploy. He sighed and told the man how the code worked.

"So, Mike, how are you going to make money from this, or are you an idealist who has some political agenda?"

"Oh, it's money I'm after."

"So, how do you get paid?"

"It's like blackmail. Sort of what you're doing with me now. I find a target, demonstrate what the code can do, and then threaten to wipe out all their files unless they pay me. If they don't pay, I wipe them out and move to the next target."

"Can't they find the code and remove it?"

"I thought of that." Mike was starting to enjoy bragging about his cleverness and Bob poured him another Scotch. Mike found that this one tasted better.

"And?"

"The code has a special routine built in. If anyone other than me attempts to access it or remove it, the delete function is triggered. They try to remove the code and they end up with a destroyed computer."

"So, who is your first target?"

"I'm not going to say."

Mike then set out an expectation which was well below what he really planned, hoping that it would result in Mr. Mystery losing interest.

"I want to start with something small by demanding one hundred thousand euros. When I see how well it works and what the glitches are, I'll solve them before I make a bigger strike. But enough of this. I'm prepared to offer you ten percent of the take. That's not negotiable."

Mike had planned this deception and he could tell the man was annoyed by the small sum involved. He smiled inwardly.

"Who do you expect to demand this ransom from?" The man in the mask was not deterred.

"I told you, I'm not revealing that. But it'll be a small bank, in a foreign country."

He saw that the man had expected something like this.

The warmth of the Scotch was having an effect on Mike and resulted in his anger growing.

"So I've told you about the code and what it does, and I still don't know who the hell you are. Hiding behind a bloody mask."

The man nodded and Mike expected there was a smile on his face behind the mask.

"My name doesn't matter, but what I want to know is how you plan to collect the money."

This was still a dilemma for Mike, and it was clear that the blackmailer had recognized this flaw in his plan.

"Haven't finalized that yet. Probably wired offshore."

"That's an area where I may be able to help."

"How?"

The man leaned forward. "The funds can be remitted to an offshore account in a country that prides itself on privacy. Privacy from the authorities.

The initial transfers can be tracked, but subsequent transfers out can't. When the bank receives the funds, they'll transfer them to another bank in another country and they'll become impossible to track."

Mike pressed him for details, but the man in the mask talked in vague terms. The hacker wondered if the man knew what he was talking about.

"Mike, this is complex stuff, and it's not cheap to set up this type of operation." Then he paused and added, "Actually, one hundred thousand euros will be as hard to hide as one million, and our laundering costs will be the same. Let's go for one million. One million euros."

Since this had been the number Mike had originally decided on, he nodded. The partnership was starting to make more sense. They had not agreed on the masked man's share yet, but that could wait. Over time, there would be enough loot for each of them.

Mike raised another issue. "I am a little short at the moment. Is there a chance of an advance of some money while I get it all set up?"

―――――∞―――――

"Ching. You're up."

Each Monday, Purple Frog held a scheduled meeting to review progress and determine priorities for going forward. Today, Silvia Lewis, the organization's director, called on the lead of Purple Frog's hacker team to report on the activities of his group.

"Things are good, Silvia. The two new Iranian hackers are doing well. They're committed and tenacious. They've infiltrated the Iranian infrastructure effectively and the intelligence they have come up with allows us to compromise another three or four senior government officials in Iran and a military general. Years back, you told me that most people interested in power had dirty little secrets, and you were right. We've proven that time and time again."

Alan Harlan, head of operations, looked up from the laptop on which he was taking notes. "I spent some time with your newbies and I like them. Any concerns?"

"None, other than getting them to take breaks and go home at night."

Ching Tong smiled, but he remembered his findings about the malware and the comment from BigCat49.

"One other thing. I spend a lot of time checking into hacker chat sites and last week I found an interesting mention about introducing a piece of malware, perhaps on a major scale. It might be included in an upgrade to one of the popular apps and I have one of the newbies looking into it. He's currently spending time checking the code in updates over the past few months. He hasn't found anything yet."

There was a knock on the conference room door and Silvia could see through the glass one of the new hackers looking flustered.

"Come in, Farid."

The hacker entered the conference room and stood looking at the Purple Frog team leaders, including his boss Ching Tong. He was shaking and nervous.

"Farid, take a seat. Relax and take a big breath." Lewis motioned to an empty seat at the end of the conference table. "Now, since you know the rules about 'no interruptions' to this weekly meeting, you must have something important that can't wait."

"My computer just died."

Ching Tong was embarrassed by his team member and annoyed that the man had broken one of the Frogs' rules. "Computers don't just die. What did you do?"

"I was looking for the possible malware you told me about and I think I found it, but just as I did so, my screen went blank. While the computer hardware looks okay, all the data, programs, OS, everything is gone."

"You didn't have it connected to our network, did you?"

"No. But everything is gone."

Lewis saw the severity of what had happened. "Ching, how could the malware have infiltrated our systems? How could it get through our cybersecurity measures?"

"Good question. The lead I was following suggested it may be piggybacked with some normal software upgrade. If that was a ubiquitous software app, every computer on the planet might have the malware already installed."

Silvia already had too many cases ongoing and did not want to add another.

"Scary, but this is outside Purple Frog's mission. The FBI or some other policing agency should handle this."

"But if it can do what it seems to be able to, it could be weaponized," Ching Tong replied.

Silvia sighed, "That would be within our mission. Put some effort into this but come back to me if it looks like anything other than just ransomware."

Chapter Seven

The day after he met the hacker, Jeff Ayling sat at his desk and was more excited than he had been in years. Banks had always been difficult to work with, and the thought of collecting one million euros from one of these sent a tremor of pleasure through his overweight body. Recently, his company's bank, one of the UK big four, had started insinuating they might be calling his outstanding loans based on his company's recent results. *They'll always lend you money if you can prove you don't need it, but when you need it, they are "missing in action,"* he thought.

His mind switched to money laundering to support Young's ransomware attack and he shook his head. He had assured the hacker that he had expertise in this field, but he did not.

His company had only one brief experience with the approach when Ayling Industries had used an offshore bank in the Isle of Man for parking profits from one of his company's overseas subsidiaries. They'd used this to avoid U.K. taxation. They had not evaded taxes, but had used legal loopholes to avoid paying what was due. Since tax avoidance was not illegal, it made sense. It was ethically wrong, but businesses across the world often employed a loose set of ethics. He had not crossed the line and had decided that avoidance was legitimate.

His finance director, a God-fearing man, prided himself on his honesty and integrity. He'd objected to the scheme, but Ayling had persisted and finally persuaded him. The finance director had implemented the approach and was the only one with the experience of doing so. However, with the man's blatant morality, using his expertise for the ransomware scheme was not an option.

Ayling was at a loss on how to proceed, but then remembered that he had met a freelance consultant in London when they were setting up the Isle of Man bank account. Ayling looked up the man's contact details from his Rolodex, located the name—James Atherton—and called him.

"James, it's Jeff Ayling. Don't know if you remember me, but we met a few years back and you helped set up Primous Incorporated in Douglas. I'm going to be down in London this week,"—this was a lie—"and I'd like to meet to discuss a few ideas I have."

"Jeff, old boy, of course I remember you. Delighted. How about Wednesday evening? Say, nine o'clock at my club?" He mentioned one of the half dozen or so private clubs on Pall Mall and Ayling accepted the invitation. It was clear that the meeting did not include dinner.

The club was founded in 1836, and until 1981 permitted only men to be members or even guests. It had a plethora of rooms where the members met, discussed their lives, played cards, and made deals when discretion and secrecy were fundamental. The members were older than some other clubs, with a median age of over sixty across all the three thousand members. A rumor had circulated that, since many members would doze off while reading the daily papers, stewards would check the date on the paper being read to determine if the member had likely expired. There were a few accommodations for members visiting from outside London, but since Ayling was not a member, he stayed at a hotel nearby.

Just before nine, Ayling arrived at the club and was met in the foyer by James Atherton, who led the way to a nearly deserted lounge room. He motioned to a couple of highbacked leather armchairs in the corner.

"Drink, Jeff?" he asked as they settled.

Ayling nodded and Atherton summoned a steward who was standing nearby. They placed their orders and the steward, a man probably in his late seventies, shuffled off.

Ayling looked his host over. Atherton's suit was a made-to-measure from, probably, a Saville Row tailor, and although Jeff was wearing one of his best suits, an off-the-rack Charles Tyrwhitt suit in a dark blue, he saw this paled when compared with that of his host. He noticed a faint smell of an exotic aftershave—was the smell cedar? The man had freshly shaved before the meeting.

"How's your health, Jeff? You look well."

"Yes. I am. Working as hard as ever, but can still get out to the golf course a few times a week."

Ayling saw that Atherton had done his homework and researched the current state of Ayling Industries when the man did not ask directly how the business was progressing.

They chatted about golf and the policies of the political parties in the United Kingdom, as well as the difficulties that Brexit had brought on many businesses. Ayling realized this was a non-threatening way to ask about his company and changed the subject. Then Atherton, obviously tired of the small talk, asked, "So, how can I help, Jeff?"

The drinks arrived and Ayling took a sip. "When we last met, you hinted that you sometimes provided services which went beyond those considered strictly legal."

Atherton faked a look of surprise at Ayling's words. "All the services that I provide are legal. But what do you have in mind?"

Jeff Ayling leaned forward and lowered his voice. "I need to provide a path for transferring a sum of money without people being able to trace where it went. I want to have access to it and be able to use it without detection. It's not really money-laundering, just hiding some assets."

"Sounds like money laundering to me, Jeff."

"You can't help?"

"I didn't say that." He leaned closer. "Something like this is fairly straightforward but expensive. How large a sum are we talking about?"

"There will be several transactions, the first being one million euros and the others being considerably higher amounts."

"That seems significantly out of Ayling Industries' league."

"It's a new partnership I've made."

Atherton did a few mental calculations. "Okay. I believe I can help."

"How would it work?"

"We'll use a standard approach, but we'll need to customize the details. These types of transactions risk a lot of attention—Special Branch, the Inland Revenue, the American FBI, or even the U.S. Treasury. There'll need to be nuances and complexities that would be unnecessary if you were just hiding funds from a wife in a divorce case. In a divorce situation, we can take a simpler approach."

He took a sip of this drink.

"If the first transfer is only one million euros, it's small enough that the authorities won't put a lot of effort into it. If your next transaction is for, say, one billion, they'll pay a lot more attention. We'll set up the first with all the safeguards we need for the subsequent ones."

"So, how will it work?"

"I'll set up a string of accounts in countries that thrive on banking secrecy. One of those used to be Switzerland, but after the U.S. put pressure on them a decade ago, and they provided information about a number of their accounts, they lost all credibility. Nowadays, we use the Cayman Islands, the BVI—that's the British Virgin Islands—Turks and Caicos, Panama, and a string of others."

He motioned to the steward for a second round of drinks.

"The funds would be transferred by wire to the first bank, say in the BVI. That transaction can be easily tracked by the authorities over the normal financial networks." Atherton took another sip of his drink. "The funds will then be transferred on in several smaller transactions over a few weeks to other banks in other havens. These banks, in turn, will transfer the funds to other banks and countries, splitting up the amounts and varying the dates of transfer."

Ayling asked the question uppermost on his mind. "How do I access the funds?"

"Ownership of the accounts in each bank will be held by local companies we'll set up for this purpose. Legally, these will be at arm's length from your control." He swirled the dregs left in his glass. "In reality, they'll be administered by nominees who will do what you want them to." The steward arrived with their next round of drinks.

"From these distributed funds, you'll be able to buy real estate, yachts, whatever you want. Most of the flats built in London in the past twenty years were funded with laundered money and are owned by companies controlled by Russian oligarchs. The authorities know the game they're playing, but identifying the actual owners is tricky, and the U.K. authorities have turned a blind eye to it."

Ayling wanted to take notes, but knew the risk of committing any of this conversation to paper.

As an afterthought, Atherton added, "Each bank will set up a few debit cards through popular U.S. banks to allow easy spending of some of the funds. We'll need to set up the bank accounts and incorporate the companies across all these countries. The banks, local law firms, and nominees will take a hefty percentage of the transaction value for the first tranche of funds, but we need the right infrastructure and it'll be good for the subsequent transactions."

Atherton sat back in his chair and tapped his fingers together. Ayling mirrored the action and then Atherton spoke again.

"Before advising you fully, I need to know more details. You need to trust me and tell me everything. Firstly, where is this money coming from? Are you planning to rob a bank?"

"Yes."

"Oh."

They talked in low voices for another hour as Ayling shared some details of the delete code and the ransomware operation. He refused to identify the hacker. In return, Atherton explained the intricacies of the likely laundering arrangement and then returned to the target for the ransomware attack.

"Which bank will you target?"

Ayling did not want to reveal that he did not know this detail, so he said, "My little secret, old boy."

A little after 11:00 p.m., Jeff Ayling left the club. It was raining as he hailed a cab in Pall Mall and returned to his hotel in Knightsbridge. It had been an exciting night and he had a warm feeling that the delete code arrangement would work out and make him immeasurably rich.

Chapter Eight

On his return to Bradford, Ayling met with the hacker again in a hotel room, but in a different hotel. His secretary, Jane, made the booking and he saw that she suspected him of using these accommodations to enjoy a secret triste. Ayling had always been a bachelor, and while he had enjoyed a dozen affairs over the years, he had never relished the idea of a wife and children. He had devoted himself to his business, the golf course, and single malt Scotch, and did not see the point of family life. His younger brother was married with children, including two sons, so the Ayling bloodline would be continued.

Before leaving for the meeting, Ayling asked Jane to call Bob up to his office.

When he arrived, Ayling said, "Bob, thanks for your efforts with this hacker thing, but I'll take over now. I don't need you to burden yourself further."

Bob looked at him and Ayling saw venom in the man's eyes.

"I also want to thank you in a more quantifiable manner," Ayling said. He withdrew an envelope from his desk drawer and handed it to the janitor.

He watched as Bob resisted the urge to open the package and check the contents.

"There's one hundred pounds in there, Bob. You've done a nice job and deserve a nice reward."

He could tell that Bob had expected more, but the man was just a janitor and Ayling believed his payment more than generous.

This time, when he met the hacker, he was not wearing his mask nor his hat, and to Mike's first question, he answered, "My name if Jeffrey Ayling. You can look me up. We now know each other, and going forward, we need to trust each other. I'll never snitch on you, and you had better not snitch on me. We have a mutual interest in keeping our operation a secret. We can both make out like bandits." He paused, then laughed. "Yes, like bandits. Because that's what we are. Aren't we?"

Young shared in the joke.

Over the next hour, Ayling explained the broad aspects of the money laundering scheme.

"One thing, Mike," Ayling told him. "This operation is complex and has a lot of moving parts. It will be expensive."

"How much?"

"The set-up and running the first sum through the system will cost about five hundred thousand euros." Ayling knew this was going to be a shock to the hacker.

"Bloody hell!" Mike gasped. "What on earth for? I can set up a bank account in town for nothing, and the bank might even give me some incentive to do so. I expected it would be expensive, but this is half the take."

Ayling nodded in understanding. "Banks down in the islands provide a service by hiding the cash. They save companies and individuals millions on taxes, and they charge accordingly. As I've explained, we also need law firms to set up the shell companies, company nominees, and to pay off government officials. And there's a lot of countries involved. And a lot of people who need to be paid."

"But that's half the take," he repeated.

"Mike, old boy, these are all set-up costs. The next sum we channel through will cost a trivial amount, and we plan for that to be significantly larger. We'll make it back. Trust me."

"Mr. Ayling, why don't I demand a ransom of two million euros?"

Ayling sympathized with the young hacker. Since he had entered Mike's life, each new exchange had diminished the amount of cash that Mike would see. He knew that Mike understood that further activities would provide an unlimited flow of cash, but he had set his heart on the first million, which had now reduced to a few hundred thousand.

"No," said Ayling. "I'm told one million is a threshold. If you target a foreign bank, the American FBI will review the case. However, they won't take an interest on a sum of one million or less, but will do so on higher amounts—even one euro over."

"But—"

" I know, you think the target bank, whoever it is, won't report the incident, but we can't be sure of that."

Ayling had brought a bottle of Scotch with him. It was a different single malt than the one he had brought to the earlier meeting. It was from a little-known distillery and held a pride of place in Ayling's personal cellar. He poured a round for the two of them.

"Let's test the system first with a million euros and iron out any kinks before we move to higher sums."

Mike nodded. It made sense.

"So, are you going to tell me which bank you have targeted?" Ayling asked.

"No. I'm not very savvy in business, but it's my delete code and my ransomware scheme. And everyone else seems to be taking over. I need some control in this gig, so the target stays my secret. Let me know where I should have them wire the money."

"I don't like it."

Mike pouted.

"I know," he said. "But you haven't told me all the details of you and your London mate's chain of companies, bank accounts, or even countries. I could end up being screwed by you people. Only I can send the delete command, and that's my leverage. I'm keeping the target to myself."

"All right, Mike. This is now over to you. Let me know when they have transferred the funds."

Although Ayling wanted to know the target, not knowing might be less risky. If something went wrong, he would be able to claim ignorance and limit his exposure. If it all worked out, he would have the keys to the kingdom and could take whatever amounts he wanted. Young had no way of assessing the net amount available, nor would he be able to access it without Ayling's help. In his calculations, he had already subtracted the money he'd paid to his janitor.

When he returned to his flat, Mike Young continued his research into his target, the First Bank of Cyprus. This time, he focused on identifying the person responsible for their safeguards against cyber-attacks. It was not easy. Surprisingly, the man — or woman — did not participate in the various cybersecurity groups worldwide, but eventually, Mike tracked him down through LinkedIn. He was a man with an Eastern European name.

Mike used one of his VPN accounts to route an email to the man through a chain of ten servers across five countries so that tracing the origin was impossible even for someone with much better skills than the Eastern European. In the email, Mike stated that he had the ability to delete all the data from the bank's systems unless money was paid. He requested a response.

The security manager replied several hours later, no doubt after attempting to track the message, with a flat refusal to the ransom request.

Dear hacker. Our systems are better than your hacking. Answer is "no."

As Mike read the short reply, it was clear that the manager was not taking his demand seriously.

I want one million euros, or I'll delete all your files, he replied in a follow up email.

He could almost hear the manager laughing at the small amount, and then received a reply that reflected humor at his request.

I'll talk to our bookkeeper and put in a petty cash voucher.

Mike replied,

You'll need to get my next message on another computer.

Mike accessed his code's dashboard, and having copied the IP address and the individual identification of the security manager's computer, he pasted this into his dashboard and clicked the button labelled "Delete."

He waited fifteen minutes and then initiated a new email thread with the IT manager, who had taken Mike's advice and logged back in on another computer after his previous screen had gone dark and his effort to restore it had proven useless.

Not joking! I can do this to every computer in your bank. Check your backup. It's gone, too, Mike keyed.

After a brief pause, Mike received a reply.

Hacker, do you know who you are dealing with?

Mike replied, *Of course. One million is petty cash.*

The reply was almost instantaneous.

One million is petty cash for us, but do you know who you are stealing it from?

The exchange surprised Mike. It was obvious that he was missing something, but he persisted.

Remit the money within the next two hours or I'll destroy half of your computers.

His reply was what Mike had expected.

I'll check with management.

To make the point, Mike sent a delete command to the computer the security manager had been using.

Two hours later, Mike reinitiated the email link. When he did so, the security manager keyed in, *Okay. We'll pay. Where do you want the funds sent?*

It seemed too easy, but Mike could not see any trickery and sent over the codes for the transfer to a bank in the BVI.

He contacted Ayling and told the businessman that the remittance was on its way.

Ayling had advanced him one thousand pounds so he could afford to go to the local liquor store and buy some beer. He'd bought two dozen bottles of a premium beer he had never been able to afford previously, and took them back to his flat where he started work on software development of his video game.

Ayling was a happy man. He found Mike's "gig" and its implied path to unlimited wealth provided him with more excitement than he had enjoyed in decades. Perhaps ever. He was now certain that it would make him a very rich man.

Initially he had seen the caper helping his company. He'd planned to inject the cash into Ayling Industries and save it from bankruptcy. Now, he had changed his mind. He would not use the funds that way, but would allow the bankruptcy to run its course. He would depart from the bleak north country climate of Britain, taking the ransomware funds with him, and live somewhere with more sun and greater, year-round warmth. Perhaps a tax-free tropical island. One with great golf courses. He might even buy an island with its own golf course. But that would all be later. Now, there was work to be done moving to the next target where the real money would be.

He confirmed that the funds had been received in Tortola and called Mike to inform him. He asked a question that had been on his mind. "So, which bank was it?"

Mike told him, "The First Bank of Cyprus."

"A bank in Cyprus?"

"Yes."

"And were there any problems?"

"None. Although the geezer I spoke with kept asking me if I knew who I was dealing with."

"Strange."

Ayling began to develop a bad feeling about their target. He called Atherton when he had hung up with the hacker and told the Londoner of their success. Atherton was delighted and congratulated him. Then Ayling broke the mood of euphoria by asking him if he knew anything about the First Bank of Cyprus.

"What about that bank, Jeff?"

"That was the one we ripped off."

Atherton exploded, "Are you insane?"

"What do you mean?"

"That bank's owned by a string of offshore companies with direct links back to the Russian government and the Russian mafia. Your clever little hacker has just stolen from some of the scariest people on the planet."

Chapter Nine

It was a Friday evening and Purple Frog was finishing up a busy week. Michael McKnight, head of Field Operations, had just returned from a trip to Russia where he had finalized recruitment of a senior member of the Russian military.

The story had started when a rumor reached Purple Frog that a nuclear warhead from Russia's arsenal was being sold by a Russian general to a terrorist group in Syria. Ching Tong's people had hacked into the general's Telegram account and decrypted messages between him and the head of the terrorists, revealing that a sum of three million euros had been agreed with half to be paid in advance. It was clear that the transaction was not between the terrorists and the Russian government but was a side deal with the Russian general, and the funds were directed to his private offshore account.

The Purple Frog hackers had traced the first payment of one and a half million euros and then diverted it to a Frog-controlled account in another country. When the general had checked to ensure that the deposit had been received, he'd discovered it hadn't been. The general believed the terrorists were trying to cheat him and refused to ship the bomb. The terrorists had remitted the money, so they'd assumed the Russian was trying to scam them. Each blamed the other for the discrepancy and the lack of trust which had been there from the beginning of the interchange blossomed into a feud between the two men. Neither had skilled cyber resources that would have allowed them to track the flow of funds, and the chain of banks that had made the various transfers were not prepared to release details.

Thinking that they were being cheated, the terrorists had initiated a scheme to collect the bomb anyway. They'd sent a team to Russia to collect the nuclear device, or, if that was not possible, to reclaim the money. McKnight and Ching Tong had fabricated messages between the two groups, adding fuel to their fire of mistrust. The result was an armed conflict and a shootout between the terrorist squad and the general's men, with several fatalities on each side. The bomb had remained in Russia and the money with Purple Frog.

Ching Tong had also sent messages to the general's superiors, laying out details of the scheme, and subsequently the general was arrested. He was quietly convicted of crimes against the state and was already rotting in a high security prison a thousand miles from Moscow.

The general's superior wanted the transaction and the disloyalty of his general kept secret, and this laid him open to exploitation by Purple Frog, who threatened to reveal the plot and his role in hiding it. Purple Frog now had another compromised Russian senior officer, as well as the one and a half million euro transfer.

"Good trip, Michael?" Silvia asked,. She met with Harlan, McKnight, and Ching Tong at 6:00 p.m., as was their custom each Friday.

"Pretty uneventful, thanks."

Silvia removed several bottles and glasses from her corner cabinet.

"I wish you guys all had the same taste in booze. I have to cater separately for each of you. Tyler and Liz are out today, so I can leave the bourbon and the Malbec in the cupboard."

She poured a Talisker Storm, a single malt Scotch, for Alan, a tequila for Michael, a vodka and tonic for Ching Tong, and a Sauvignon Blanc for herself.

The Friday evening gathering had become a ritual, a time when the senior members of the froggie teams met and talked less formally, often about their personal lives.

"How is Brian doing?" Alan asked, referring to Silvia's husband.

"He's good. Ever since we pushed him into his podcasts, he's moved on from the collapse of his hedge fund. That marketing consultant guy Jason set up is doing a great job managing the business side, and Brian just concentrates on the financial markets, writing about them and then creating the podcasts. He's as happy as a clam." She clinked glasses with Harlan. "How is married life?"

"It's great. Not a lot of change from when we were just living together, but I think Jess finds it more stable and seems to be happy."

"What about your work here at Purple Frog? In the last few missions, she's seen more of you in action. Does she have a problem with that?"

"No. Actually, she seems to get a kick out of it. It's a vicarious blast for her. When we were on our honeymoon, she faced a particularly dangerous situation, and I have never seen her more animated."

"And Purple Frog's secrets?"

"They're safe with her. I don't tell her much, no matter how hard she grills me."

"And Avery, Michael?" she asked, turning to McKnight.

"My wife is just fine. She knows a little of what I do, but she takes the view that what she doesn't know won't hurt her."

Ching Tong took a gulp of his vodka and tonic. "I'm pissed," he said.

Alan laughed. "Drunk already?"

"Not British pissed. American pissed. Annoyed."

Silvia sipped her Sauvignon Blanc. "What's up?"

Ching Tong put his drink down. "Jess is stunning. And Michael, your wife Avery is an absolute beauty as well. I need to find someone. I never even go on dates."

"It'll have to be outside Frog, Ching," Silvia said, reminding the hacker of Purple Frog's policy regarding fraternization.

"And that's the problem. I spend fifteen hours a day or more here, so I don't have much free time. And, if I go out with someone, they ask me what I do and I have to start a relationship by lying to them. And if I appear depressed on a date, I can't tell the girl that's because we're facing some global crisis that the public doesn't know about." He sighed. "So it's not likely I shall ever find anyone."

Alan nodded. He understood the problem, but had been lucky with Jess. They had started their involvement before he'd joined Purple Frog, but if he had not met her when he had, the pressures of running operations at the clandestine organization may well have put him in the same boat Ching was now in. In their early days, after he had joined Silvia and relocated to the United States from London, his relationship with Jess had been tenuous, even when they started living together. He had not been able to share most of what he did, and this had caused suspicion on Jess's part.

Thinking about the point Ching had brought up, he decided to talk to Silvia about it in private. In the earlier days, many lifelong relationships and marriages had been between colleagues at their place of employment. In recent years, fraternization had become criticized and unacceptable. Maybe Purple Frog should relax its rules.

That night, Alan raised the idea with Jess.

She sipped her Chardonnay and moved her head to the right, which told Alan she understood the issue and had an opinion on it. *I know her body language so well now,* he thought.

"I think allowing fraternization is a great idea," she said. "Everyone needs relationships, and one of those needs to be more than just being friends."

Alan sipped his Scotch. "But, if two of the froggies start a relationship and it turns sour, it can affect their interaction at work. One of the two might even feel the need to resign."

"Do you have a good HR manager?"

"Yes."

Jess held out her glass for a refill. "Then he, or she, should be able to develop and release a policy that'll work. Anyway, what's for dinner?"

The following day, Alan met with Silvia and put forward his ideas.

"I've been thinking about what Ching Tong was saying and I think we should change our fraternization policies."

"So, we're going to say that making out in house is okay?"

"You know that's not what I'm saying. The froggies find it difficult having outside relationships, and we prohibit those within the organization. The policy that I'm advocating won't encourage internal relationships, but will say that we understand that attraction happens, and we don't want to stand in the way. A relationship would be permissible providing it's made known to the HR Manager, who will resolve any conflicts that affect Purple Frog. She'll keep it secret and there will be no repercussions."

"Let me think about it. I'll give you an answer tomorrow."

The next day, Janice Price, who had previously held a Human Resources position in a security group in Google, but now worked for Silvia at Purple Frog, met with her boss. Shortly afterwards, she sent out an email to all staff.

The subject was "Intracompany Relationships," and the body of the message discussed the issue and reminded the staff of the current policy of "no in-house relationships." It went on to acknowledge the dilemmas the froggies faced and announced a change in that policy. Relationships would now be permitted providing they did not interfere with the day-to-day operations of the organization, and to ensure a "no conflict" situation, relationships of this type were to be shared, on a strictly confidential basis, with Janice, as head of HR. If necessary, to avoid either actual or perceived conflict, she would make recommendations of changes in reporting lines.

Ching Tong looked at his screen, read the email, and whistled. A half hour later, he ambled over to the profiling group and walked up to the Spanish profiler, Ginny Krangle.

"Feel like a drink tonight?"

She was reading the email and looked up. "No fucking way, Ching."

Chapter Ten

Milos Kurbanova, the CEO of the First Bank of Cyprus, was furious. How could some idiot blatantly extort money from his bank? His head of security had explained the severity of the threat and had shown him the dead computers, which indicated that the hacker could inflict the type of damage he'd asserted. He was filled with fear of losing all their records and the impact this would have on his small but important customer base. It was daunting. If the hacker could do what he said—and he had shown that he probably could—fortunes would be lost and Kurbanova would suffer a long and painful death. His customers were not a gentle group, and did not react well to things not going to their liking.

After his fear quietened, it was replaced by anger. He was amazed at how stupid the hacker was not to realize that the bank was a front for holding funds on behalf of the Russian president, as well as many of the oligarchs and Russian mob bosses. But he faced a dilemma. If he revealed the theft, it would likely result in his head being separated from his gangly body, probably after some other parts had been painfully removed. He shuddered at the thought.

He was an intelligent man and had always adopted an optimistic attitude, so he tried to view this catastrophe as, perhaps, an opportunity.

The hacker had code that could attack computers, and this might be able to be harnessed and used to the bank's advantage. However, to do so would require locating and capturing the hacker. When he did this, Kurbanova would persuade him to apply his skills for the benefits of the bank and its clients. Recovering the money was important since not recovering it would be a sign of weakness, but making use of the hacker's skill would allow for much better long-term returns. It could make a lot of money, and making money was the gold standard for the bank and its clients.

It is said that bad news travels faster than good news, and within an hour of the Cyprus bank transferring the ransom to the BVI, a junior member of the bank's programming staff posted a message over Telegram to the dark web, marveling at the ransom attack and the ability of the hacker to delete all the data and software from the target machines. He spoke in specific terms about the attack, but did not reveal the identity of the bank or the country in which it was located.

A few minutes after he had made his post, he received an email addressed to all members of the bank. Management made it clear that the attack and its success was to be kept secret to avoid having the bank's customers rattled by the intrusion. It was too late, and the programmer realized his foolishness and hoped no one would notice. He made a silent prayer not to be found out and admonished.

Ching Tong focused his attention on the malware and its dangers discovered by Purple Frog's newest hacker, Farid. One of his actions was to recalibrate a vast set of bots that he'd used to comb the broader web and the dark web searching for references based on a set of keyword phrases. Almost immediately, one of these triggered a notification and Ching Tong saw the post from the Cyprus bank's programmer.

He called a meeting with Alan Harlan and explained what he had found.

"Alan, there has been a ransomware attack. PCs have had all their software and data deleted, and it looks like a hacker extracted a million euros to prevent further systems from being compromised."

"Who was the victim?"

"I don't know that. The programmer reporting the breech guarded that well."

"Country?"

"Looks like Europe somewhere."

"When was the money paid?"

"I have a range of dates within a few days of one another."

"Can we trace the transaction?"

"I can't, but I'll bet that Tyler and his people can."

Tyler Waylon had joined Purple Frog in the early days after a successful career in the U.S. Treasury tracking down money laundering activities of the South American drug cartels. He had developed a wide range of techniques and contacts, which allowed him and his team to track monetary transfers. In some cases, his team worked with Ching Tong's group, intercepting money flows and diverting them to Purple Frog accounts. One of Waylon's people, Patricia Rand, had been responsible for hijacking the payment from the Syrian terrorist organization to the Russian general.

Harlan briefed Waylon on what Ching had been able to find out and Tyler started his team searching for the initial transaction, which they assumed would have been a wire transfer of the full one million euros.

Patricia Rand undertook the search and in less than an hour, she called her boss.

"Bingo!" she said.

"You found it?"

"I think so. The First Bank of Cyprus."

"Very interesting." He put a call in to Harlan as Rand started to look for transactions in smaller denominations leaving the BVI bank over the next week or so.

Waylon, Rand, and Harlan met, and Patricia took the floor. Waylon gestured that he wanted to make a point. "Before you start, Patricia, there's something we need to be aware of."

All eyes turned to the spectacled man, who had the appearance of a corporate accountant.

"Whoever did this is very smart but very naïve. The First Bank of Cyprus is a front for the Russians, and they will not take kindly to being ripped off. I believe we can expect they will not report the loss, but will institute a search using their own people or some hired contractors. This hacker may have a short time to spend his ransom money."

He nodded to Rand to start her findings. She addressed Harlan. "Well, Alan, I can't be sure of all the transfers, but my algorithm has a good take on the main paths of the money. It's a rather small amount."

"One million euros is rather small?"

"Yes. Normally these laundering schemes are for hundreds of millions or billions, and this looks like a first. It's not one using an established chain. It looks like a new chain was set up for this one alone."

"Okay, go on."

"The scheme is quite sophisticated, but including the complexity they need for implementing it is costly. Laundering one billion wouldn't cost much more than it would for one million, so the percentage lost by the hacker in this case is huge. For that reason, I think they took a few shortcuts and that helped me trace them. There is about five hundred thousand euros held in about twenty accounts across eight banks. The other half million was probably collected as fees by the banks, law firms, and so on."

"Can you identify the overall owner?"

"For that, we need to hack into one of the banks at the end of the chain, and I have Ching already working on that."

"Where is that bank?"

"St. Vincent."

"St. Vincent?"

"The main island in St. Vincent and the Grenadines. It's a small tax haven and attracts a lot less attention than the better-known ones like the Caymans, the BVI, and Panama."

"And you think they know the identity of the hacker?"

"I don't know that, but they will be able to identify whoever set up the chain of accounts and who has control of the funds. Normally the last bank in the chain is where the launderer starts and works back from there."

"Nice job, Patricia. Let's get on with it." Harlan left the conference room.

Atherton was a worried man. He knew that the First Bank of Cyprus would not accept the theft lightly. Even though it was only one million euros of its clients' money, the heist would anger some very vicious customers. The bank had not made anything public about the hack, so it was likely they had their own thugs on the trail of the hacker. If they managed to follow the trail of fund transfers to the end, they would be able to identify him. From there they would want to know his client, and he shuddered at the thought of that interchange. Throwing Ayling under the bus did not bother him, but if they asked him about the hacker, he would not be able to tell them anything, and that would result in a tricky situation.

He considered running, but knew that when he was identified, the thugs would track him down wherever he was. *And I did all this for a paltry one hundred thousand pounds*, he thought. The big scores that were expected to follow were probably now in jeopardy.

He walked into his library, poured himself a large Cognac, and settled down in a leather winged armchair.

How could I have been so bloody stupid?

Chapter Eleven

Within a few days, Ching Tong's people had hacked into the computers of the St. Vincent bank. The bank's computers were protected by a robust security system which had been installed by an experienced cyber defense contractor from Miami. When installed, it had been state-of-the-art, and offered excellent protection with a superior firewall and other anti-hacking software. However, while the contractor had implemented a sound set of measures, the system had not been kept up to date and was vulnerable to newer hacking techniques. Ching's team found entry to the systems straightforward.

Ching Tong had assigned Anna Ivanov, one of his team who had previously held a senior systems position at Kaspersky, the antivirus software firm, to the task. "Got it. I'm in," she said quietly as she gained access.

"What have you found?"

Ivanov worked for an hour exploring the file structures and accessing the various folders in the systems, and then turned to Ching Tong and smiled.

"I've got it all. The most useful doc is a diagram of the whole laundering strategy. The countries, the banks, the account numbers, the new or fake ownership companies, nominees, the amount transferred, and the schedule of the transfers. Also, the end client. Its someone called James Atherton."

They ran the name by Patricia Rand and she smiled. "Our old friend. He's been setting up and running this type of scheme for years now, but the U.S. and U.K. authorities have never been able to catch him. He's a Brit and lives in London."

Ching said, "I guess field ops can go to London and find out who's behind the scheme."

"Is it even worth it for this small amount?" Patricia queried.

———⦻———

Ching requested a meeting with Harlan, who called in Michael McKnight and laid out a plan of action.

Ching Tong was excited. "Alan, we really need to jump on this."

"Why? It sounds like a rather petty crime. It's the sort of thing the police should tackle. Let's bundle up what we have found and send it on to Scotland Yard or the FBI and let them run with it."

Ching Tong exhaled loudly "I think that's the wrong call, Alan." The hacker then proceeded to spell out his rationale for Purple Frog investigating the ransomware attack, and after several minutes had convinced Harlan of the potential threat beyond a simple ransomware scheme.

Harlan nodded and made his decision. "Michael, take Paul with you and go to St. Vincent. Do what you must to find out what they know. Interrogating the manager there should help fill in the details not covered in our hack of the system." McKnight nodded.

"We also need to start tracking Atherton," Harlan added.

McKnight looked up from the pad where he had been taking notes. "I'll send Donna Strickland and Jeff Acton to London."

While Ching and his fellow hackers had been gaining access to the bank's files in St. Vincent through electronic means, a group of Chechens flew from Cyprus to the BVI to start their own tracking of the stolen funds.

Before leaving Nicosia in Cyprus, the Chechen team met with Milos Kurbanova.

"Listen closely to my orders," Milos told them. "Use my name and my bank's name and start with the BVI bank where we first sent the funds. Remind them of who we are and what we stand for. Also remind them of the level of business we have channeled through them over the years. Tell them they have no excuse not to tell us everything."

He looked the group's leader up and down. He was tall and well-built, with a long scar down the side of his face and unblinking brown eyes.

"You and your men look tough and dangerous. Good. Exploit that. No excuses. Find out the chain of remittances—which countries, which banks, which accounts, what amounts. Find the son-of-a-bitch who orchestrated this hit on my bank. Get the money back, but it's more important find the hacker. Do not harm him. He is valuable."

They flew to Tel Aviv, then changed planes for the flight to Miami, and then to Puerto Rico. There they boarded a small plane which deposited them at Beef Island, Tortola's airport. Over the next several days, they crisscrossed the Caribbean and interrogated six banks on different islands. They had discussions, some friendly and others threatening, and found the name and location of the bank that had set up the chain of remittances to manage the laundering operation: the St. Vincent Trust Bank in St. Vincent and the Grenadines.

The four Chechens deplaned the American Airways flight at Argyle International Airport in St. Vincent about five miles outside the territory capital, Kingstown.

Although they wore expensive suits and crisply starched white shirts with ties, the Chechens looked just what they were: thugs.

Their leader was a little shorter than his three companions at only six foot one, but they were all heavily muscled and displayed the persona of a military background. To even a casual observer, the four men were a team, although they sat separately on the American Airways flight and did not communicate with each other. The sky marshal on the flight watched them closely and was relieved when the plane landed without incident and the four disembarked.

They separately hailed taxis, which took them to the same hotel, and they checked in. The tradecraft they had used was amateur, and they could have all travelled together for all the good their half-hearted separation did to disguise their relationship.

A half hour later, they met in the leader's room and planned their next moves.

The leader spoke to them in Russian and set out the plan. "There is no time to waste. We need to find out who the hacker is, or who is running him. We'll go to the bank tomorrow and ask the man in charge. He'll tell us or regret it."

The St. Vincent Trust bank was located in a small, detached building on the outskirts of Kingstown. The building had been erected at the end of the last century and had joined others in the city, which held little linkage to the past of the originally French colony.

The Chechens took two taxis to the bank. Two of the team stood outside the building, watching for any signs of trouble, while the leader and one other entered. They walked past the security guard to a personal assistant who sat at a desk at the end of the banking chamber.

The leader said in English, "We see manager. We have appointment. We from First Bank of Cyprus."

The personal assistant, a tall, slender girl in her early thirties, smiled at the men and looked at her computer. "I'm sorry, but I don't see an appointment. Was it for today?"

"It is for any day. But now we here. So today."

She looked up and for the first time took in the aura of danger that the two men exuded. She smiled again. "I'll see if he is free."

"He free, lady."

She put a call in to her manager and a short time later, a thin, short man emerged dressed in an expensive dark gray Italian suit, a light blue sea island cotton shirt, and a navy, yellow, and white stripe silk necktie.

"I am the manager," he announced, and motioned the two Chechens into his air-conditioned office.

He looked the men up and down and the Chechen leader saw the man had assessed them as dangerous. The manager now knew that they represented the First Bank of Cyprus, an important customer and known for its illegal connections, so he was obliged to tell them anything they wanted to know. It was also clear they would not hesitate to kill him if they were not satisfied with his answers.

Once they reached the office, he said, "Gentlemen, welcome to St. Vincent and the Grenadines. How may I help you?"

Chapter Twelve

The Chechen team returned to their hotel after spending an hour with the head of the St. Vincent bank. Their leader put through a call to Kurbanova and they spoke in Russian.

"I found most of the funds, sir. Your hacker people spent a lot of the money on these slimy bankers, their lawyers, and setting up the shell companies. Most of that and the funds still in accounts will be remitted back to you."

"Fine. But more important, who is the hacker and where is he?"

"The manager here had a contact in London. His name is James Atherton."

"I know him. He's not the hacker. He's a fixer, but he probably knows who the hacker is. I'll have another team take care of him and follow the trail back to the little shit who did this to me. No one steals from me. No one steals from Russia. Did you find out who else knows about this? We need to ensure that none of this gets out."

"No one else in the chain knew much. They didn't know the background nor the contact. It was all handled from here. The manager of the bank here was the only contact with Atherton, and he set up arrangements with the other banks. No one else knew what the money was for, nor the name Atherton."

"The manager will not talk to anyone about this, right?"

"No. He is a very scared man."

"Make sure he does not talk."

"Permanently?"

"Yes."

Airport security measures prevented the Chechen team from bringing firearms with them on their trip, and their leader realized they should be armed when they revisited the bank. He called contacts he had in Nicosia and learned of a man who would be able to provide them with what they needed.

That afternoon, they took a taxi to a small, dilapidated building outside the main town and met with the man, who showed them a collection of handguns, mostly revolvers.

"Automatics not good in the heat, mon," the arms dealer explained.

The Chechen responded, "Don't like revolvers."

"I've got a few Browning 9mm, but no Glocks or other modern stuff. Anyway, as I said, they jam down here."

The Chechens had little choice, since this man seemed to be the only one who could provide what they needed. They were on the point of agreeing to purchase four handguns when the arms dealer paused.

"Hey. Just had a thought. Would you like some AK47s? I can get them tomorrow."

That evening, the team met for dinner at a small restaurant close to their hotel. Their leader chose a table where they would not be overheard, and they spoke quietly in Russian.

"As well as eliminating the bank manager, we need to destroy the computer files and any print outs. We'll collect the AK47s tomorrow morning and go to the bank after that."

"Can't we go to the beach?"

"Idiot. This is not a vacation."

They had ordered glasses of the local Sunset rum.

"This is good. I like it more than vodka."

They were relaxed, and while their bosses back in Cyprus wanted them to tie up the loose ends in St. Vincent, the team had decided that after their action at the bank, a few days extra to relax was not going to be a problem. And their expenses in this tropical island were being covered. Maybe they would get to the beach after all.

As the Chechens were negotiating with the arms dealer, another American Airlines flight from Miami arrived at the Argyle International Airport, and shortly afterwards, Michael McKnight and Paul Weber passed through immigration and headed to their hotel. Their hotel was different than the one where the Chechens were staying, but when they went out to dinner that night, the restaurant that both teams chose happened to be the same, Vee Jay's.

The Purple Frog team, dressed casually in sporting attire, arrived after the Chechens had consumed several rounds of rum and started their evening meal. As McKnight looked around the dining spot for a table where he and Weber could talk, his eyes took in the table at the rear of the restaurant where the four men sat. They were still dressed in suits and ties, looking totally out of place in this tourist resort. McKnight gestured Weber to a table in sight of the Chechens and he and his colleague took their seats. Paul Weber was facing the table in the rear.

"Paul, check out the suits at the back," McKnight said.

"Saw them. Are they really businessmen?"

"That's what the suits say, but the people wearing them look Eastern European and military."

"Maybe they're here for the same purpose we are."

"Could be."

They ordered drinks and observed that the "suits" were ordering another round of rums and swilling them down.

"Let's wait for them to finish," McKnight said. "If they are a little drunk, which looks likely, follow them. They may be here just by coincidence, but maybe not." They ordered their own drinks and watched as the Chechens ordered yet another round.

"What you like for dinner, gentlemen?" A tall waitress smiled at the froggies and motioned to the menus they held.

"What's good?"

"Everything good here, mon,"

They ordered curried chicken and rice with green bananas and settled back, wishing they could overhear the Chechens' conversation.

McKnight rose and walked to the rear of the restaurant, looking back and forth as if trying to locate the men's room. He passed the Chechens' table at a distance but was able to pick up snippets of their conversation. He found the men's room and a few minutes later returned to his table.

"They're speaking Russian, but with Chechen accents. They are talking about a bank."

"The same one we're investigating?"

"Don't know, but that's my guess."

The Chechens were paying their bill just as the chicken and rice was being served. McKnight turned to Weber.

"I know you're hungry, but I'll have them keep it hot for you till you get back. Go find out where they're staying."

Weber scowled but rose and left the restaurant. He waited in the darkness of the tropical evening. It was a balmy seventy-six degrees with a light breeze coming off the harbor a block away, and when the Chechens emerged, they walked, staggering a little, back to their hotel. Weber followed them, being careful not to be observed, and noted that they paid no attention to checking for possible surveillance.

"Amateurs," he judged accurately.

He returned to the restaurant and found that both plates of chicken and rice were empty.

McKnight laughed at his dismay. "I was hungry, and it was really good. I'll order you another."

Weber told his boss what he had seen.

"So, what do we do, Michael?" he asked when he had finished.

"There are four of them, and I'll bet they are here to close loose ends, which probably means the staff at the bank, the files, and backups of data about the money transfers. They may have even completed their mission, but the body language tonight told me that they are still in the planning stage."

The waitress appeared and McKnight motioned to the empty plates, ordering another as well as two more drinks.

"Comin' right up, gentlemen."

After she left, McKnight leaned forward. "We'll just watch them for the time being. If—or when—they make a move, we can decide whether we want to intercept. One of us will track them and the other will visit the bank." McKnight withdrew a quarter from his pocket and tossed it in the air. "Heads or tails?"

The next day, McKnight visited the St. Vincent Trust Bank and asked to see the manager.

"Do you have an appointment, sir?"

"No, but the manager may be facing some serious threats which I can help with."

"Oh." The receptionist started to shake. She regarded the tall black man as less intimidating than the men she had met the day before, but still dangerous.

She dialed the manager's number, spoke briefly, and the door to his office opened.

"What do you people want now?" he said. It was clear that at seeing McKnight, he realized the black man was unlikely to be part of the Chechen group from the day before.

"I would like to discuss an account you have at your bank."

The manager shook his head but welcomed McKnight to his office.

They sat in two armchairs facing one another and the manager called for coffee and water for both of them.

McKnight came straight to the point. "On April twenty-second, you received a transfer of two hundred thousand dollars, which was credited to an account in the name of Ajax Financial Company.

Another for a hundred and fifty thousand dollars was received for another account a day later but for the same company. That company is new and is owned by a nominee in Jersey in the U.K."

He paused, observing the manager's reaction to this level of detail about the transactions. The manager squirmed.

"I want to confirm that the nominee links back to James Atherton."

The manager froze but said, "You know I cannot tell you anything. How you know about some transfer or other, which may or may not be real, is beyond me."

"Have the Chechens visited you yet?"

The manager's face gave him away. "Perhaps."

"They are still on the island, which probably means they're not done with you. They'll probably kill you."

The manager's black face turned paler.

McKnight noticed the nameplate on the manager's desk. "Mr. Hughes, I may be able to help, but you're going to need to help me in return."

"There are four of them and only one of you. If I feel there is a risk, I'll call the police. I have friends in the administration here and they'll protect me. Me and my family."

McKnight's smartphone rang and he looked at the screen. The call was from Weber and he picked up.

"Michael, they are just entering the bank. They're carrying AK47s. Watch out."

Outside in the banking chamber, they heard shouts from the Chechens, followed by a number of shots and screams.

McKnight had not come to the island armed, so he beckoned to the manager. "Do you have a firearm?"

"Yes. But I haven't used it in years."

"Give it to me."

The manager hesitated for a moment and then took an ancient Browning 9mm from his desk drawer and handed it to McKnight, who checked the magazine and chambered a round. He motioned the manager to move away from the line of sight to the door, which burst open. One of the Chechens entered, leveling his rifle at where he expected the manager to be sitting. He was momentarily surprised that the seat was empty and was swinging the gun around when McKnight sent a nine millimeter bullet into his brain. Michael caught the AK47 as the lifeless Chechen fell to the floor. He quickly checked the magazine, finding it full, having not yet fired a round.

A voice came from the banking chamber in Russian, asking if the man had accomplished his mission of killing the bank manager.

McKnight answered in Russian but lacked the Chechen accent. "No. Your man failed."

A second man charged through the open door and McKnight killed him with a shot to the chest. That left two.

A voice bellowed from the banking chamber, "We outnumber you and we'll kill you. Put down your weapon and come out with your hands up. I'll spare you."

McKnight replied in Russian, "Bullshit." It seemed like a standoff, but then there were two sets of double-tap shots from the chamber and Weber appeared in the doorway. "Don't shoot. It's me, Paul."

McKnight lowered his rifle.

"I'm glad you brought your Vektor, Paul." Weber holstered the ceramic handgun he had brought to the island in his luggage. McKnight, Weber, and the bank manager left the office and looked about the banking chamber. The single security guard was dead, as was the receptionist and the one teller. Other doors opened quietly from the back office and a half dozen people emerged from the various administrative offices of the small bank.

The manager called out, "Everything is fine now. Back to your desks. Luis, close the bank and wait for my further orders."

The manager and the two froggies went back into his office and he sat down, obviously devastated by the carnage of people he had known and worked with for many years.

"Whoever you are, thank you. I'm sure they would have killed everyone in the bank."

And destroyed all the records and computers, thought Michael.

The bank manager continued, "I'll call someone I know in the police force and we'll sort this out quietly. St. Vincent has a small but thriving financial services industry, and we don't want violence to impact our credibility. My friend will solve this issue and you and your colleague will be able to go back to wherever you've come from."

"Okay, but this seems to be linked to the transactions we discussed. Can you verify that Atherton's the real owner?"

"I owe you, so yes. He is the one who set up the scheme."

McKnight and Weber left the bank, packed quickly, and after checking out, took a taxi to the airport. Their flight left late afternoon, and after a night's sleep in their homes, they were back in the office early the next day.

Harlan met them for a debrief. "So, is Atherton confirmed?"

"Yes, boss. But we ran into a little problem." He proceeded to report the confrontation with the Chechens.

"You are lucky you're not both dead or in a jail in paradise."

McKnight hung his head. "We really didn't have another option."

"So, now we've confirmed Atherton. Where are Strickland and Acton?"

"They're in London and waiting for my instructions."

"Right. Have them meet with Atherton and let's follow the trail to the hacker."

Chapter Thirteen

As they sat in their small rental car in London, Jeff Acton looked at his companion, Donna Strickland, and marveled yet again that this attractive, young blonde woman was an experienced killer. Her demure looks hid her overall ruthlessness, and she had used her sensuality to distract many of the Frog's enemies before capturing or killing them.

It was late afternoon, and Acton and Strickland had located James Atherton's home, a fine townhouse in the fashionable area of Mayfair. They'd found that Atherton was not there and had settled down to await his return from work.

At about 5:00 p.m., they observed a team of men arrive and station themselves out of sight close to the house's entrance. A little later a taxi stopped outside the dwelling and a tall, well-dressed man alighted. He paid the taxi driver, withdrew a key, and moved to the front door.

"Atherton?" asked Acton.

Strickland checked a photo of their target on her smartphone.

"Yes."

Two of the waiting men emerged and confronted the fixer, and after a brief exchange, they opened the door and went inside with him. It was clear that Atherton was reluctant.

Jeff could not determine their nationality, but was sure that they displayed a military bearing. Based on McKnight's experience in St. Vincent, this pointed to them being another hit squad.

Atherton's day had been a good one. He had landed another—though small—contract for a breakaway group in Qatar, which he had not expected. As he put his key in the lock and opened his front door, two men emerged from the darkness and pushed him inside. They followed him and closed the door behind them. As the door was closing, he saw two more men taking up positions outside.

"Who the hell are you? What do you want?"

"We from First Bank of Cyprus. We want talk, Mr. Atherton."

"Oh, shit."

The leader of the Chechen team looked over at Atherton's body, which laid in a pool of blood and was oozing even more blood over a priceless, antique, silk Persian carpet.

As he and his team departed the townhouse, he placed a call to Kurbanova.

"Yes?" the banker answered.

"Atherton was not the hacker."

"I know that. So, who is the hacker?"

"He didn't know."

"He must know something. He must have had a contact. There must be a chain." Kurbanova was getting angry.

"Of course, sir. Atherton told us who his contact is. His name is Jeffrey Ayling, and he lives in Bradford. That's in the north of England."

"So, is he the hacker?"

"No. Atherton said he is just someone he dealt with. He did not know the identity of the hacker, but this Ayling does."

"Damn. Go to Bradford and find out who the hacker is. How did you leave Atherton?"

"Dead, sir."

"Good."

Donna saw the group leave the townhouse and drive away in an SUV. Atherton was not with them.

"Follow them or check on Atherton?" she asked Jeff.

"Atherton is the one we need to question, so I say we stick with him."

"If he's still alive." Donna had a strong feeling that their target would not be in a state to tell them anything, but they needed to confirm this.

She went to the front door and rang the bell. There was no reply, and her fear that Atherton was dead increased.

Acton withdrew a set of lock picks and in less than a minute had opened the door. They proceeded into the house with pistols drawn and found Atherton's body.

"They made a mess of him," Donna said, observing the multiple knife wounds that had been inflicted as they'd tortured the man. A jagged rip across his throat showed how his life had ended. "They tortured him, but there are only a few wounds, so my take is that he told them what they wanted to know, and probably early. And then they killed him."

"Did they get what they wanted?"

Donna motioned to the dead man. "Probably, and that was what we're after as well. The name and location for the hacker."

Acton looked around the living room. It was rather overcluttered, but with very expensive furnishings. None had been disturbed.

"They didn't search at all, so whatever they wanted, he gave it to them."

Donna shook her head.

"Michael thought that the Chechens he ran into in St. Vincent probably passed on Atherton's name to their boss. That team is dead so the four we saw here were another group following the chain."

"Well, we'll not find anything from him now. We're at a dead end." Jeff motioned towards the body.

———⚮———

Alan Harlan called a meeting with Ching Tong and the team he had working on the phantom code to discuss their progress with the malware.

"It's really clever stuff, Alan," Ching Tong started. "The normal antivirus software which most people use runs automatically and is just fine, but it doesn't pick up a trace of the malware. Running it doesn't trigger the code, either. Very smart."

"What have you done to locate and remove it?"

"That's the problem. Every time we get close, we trigger the code and have a dead computer on our hands. We assume it's embedded in some application, or perhaps even the operating system."

Anna Ivanov interrupted, "I don't think it's in the operating system. We've tested both Windows and IOS systems. The malware is on both, so the hacker would have had to develop two versions. That, plus the fact that Microsoft has huge cyber checking on its Windows upgrades and Apple has something similar on IOS for its Macs." She paused and then added, "My bet is on an application package."

"But we still need to check the OS," Ching Tong said. "He may have developed it for both."

There were six people in the meeting and a freewheeling interchange broke out. Harlan let them chatter for a few minutes and then interjected, "Enough. Ching, how are you tackling the problem?"

"I have each member of my team directing their attention to a specific parameter. Anna has the operating system, Nick Microsoft Office..." He spelled out the focus for each of his team members.

"The problem is that we have been burning through PCs and Macs like there is no tomorrow. We've tried all the malware removal software out there, and some from the dark web, which is more experimental. Bottom line: so far, nothing works."

"Keep trying. Hopefully you'll make a breakthrough." Alan Harlan had studied computing at the University of London, and had been a systems analyst and programmer in the early part of his career, but he knew Ching Tong and the other hackers were far better skilled to address the issue. "Good luck, everyone."

Jeff Ayling lived in a Tudor mansion in the countryside north of Bradford. Though he lived alone, he had decided many years before that he would buy and live in an impressive, large house that stated to the world that he was an important man and one of wealth. The house had four bedrooms and three reception rooms, which were laid out in a traditional Elizabethan style under a steep pitched roof built with several gables. Each room had a fireplace with a separate chimney that stretched up, far above the roofline of the mansion.

Ayling did not have live-in staff since he preferred to spend his evenings alone, or in the company of the occasional woman. He did not want servants popping in on an intimate moment asking if he wanted anything. However, during the day, he had three people, two men and a woman, who were paid by Ayling Industries and who set up his fireplaces, cleaned, tended to the grounds, and prepared his meals. Each evening, the woman cooked his dinner, and once she had served it, she departed for the night and cleared up the next day after Ayling had departed for his office or the golf course. He did not eat breakfast.

One evening, the cook prepared "Toad in the Hole," a favorite meal of his, and he had enjoyed it with a bottle of French Bordeaux. When he finished eating, he folded his napkin and brought his knife and fork together in parallel. With company or wait staff, this indicated completion of his meal, but even when alone, he followed the habit. He rose and walked the twenty feet to his main study where a fire was crackling in the grate. Throwing another log on to keep it going, he poured himself a single malt Scotch. The whisky was from the Isle of Skye and had a toasted, peaty aroma, which he savored before sipping it. He looked at a side table against the wall where he had about twenty bottles of Scotch from various distilleries, and he smiled at his hobby. *I must try a Talisker Storm tomorrow,* he thought. He crossed the room, sat in his favorite armchair, and took up a book he was reading. He sipped the amber liquid and felt relaxed and content.

His mind shifted to the ransomware that he was now party to. The first "gig," as his new hacker partner called it, had gone smoothly. The funds had been channeled through the various accounts and were now all securely held in tax havens in the Caribbean. The fears Atherton had about the bank the money had been taken from seemed behind them, and Ayling's thoughts shifted to where the next target should be and how much they would demand. *Perhaps twenty million next time. Perhaps fifty. Why not a billion?*

His thoughts were interrupted by the sound of a bell being rung. In Tudor tradition, this was at the front door of the house and indicated that someone had arrived and wanted his attention. He smiled. It was an old ship's bell made of bronze and was rung by moving a cord attached to the ringer back and forth inside the bell housing. Having an electric doorbell would be so gross, and a knocker would never be heard within the vast building.

He went to the door, opening it without thinking, and was confronted by four men wearing suits with somber ties.

"Mr. Ayling?" the lead man said in an Eastern European accent.

Chapter Fourteen

Ching Tong was not the only one to pick up the scent of the delete code.

In Shanghai, another Chinese hacker with a military rank of corporal, and working for the Cyber Offensive team of the People's Liberation Army—or Chinese military—also saw the comment by BigCat49 and later the thread about the ransomware attack. He wrote up his findings and reported this to his superior, Dang Huan.

Born in North Korea, Dang had travelled to China as part of a joint hacker program. He had married a traditional Chinese woman and had been fortunate enough to be allowed to stay in China. Dang was thirty-two and held the rank of colonel. His Cyber Offensive team numbered over a thousand hackers, mostly in their late teens.

When he heard about the malware software, he saw the potential value and decided not to follow the money, as the Purple Frog team had, but to concentrate on identifying BigCat49. He summoned a dozen officers from his battalion and ordered them to track down the phantom hacker, feeling sure this was the person who held the key to something which might have much greater value than just a method to extort money. It might even be a strategic weapon that China's head of state, President Yang, could deploy in his goal for world domination.

It took them only a few days to identify BigCat49. She was a woman in Bradford, England, called Cate Glover, and a Chinese team was dispatched to kidnap the woman, whom they assumed was the hacker who had developed the code.

A week later, as Cate was making her unsteady way back to her flat from the pub, an Asian man approached her.

"Hello. Are you Cate Glover?"

She regarded him with suspicion, not from any racial prejudice, but just as a man who had approached her late at night on a deserted street.

"Who wants to know?"

The man punched her in the jaw, sending her to the ground. Another Asian man came forward and a van pulled level with the group. A door opened and they threw her into the vehicle, where a third man placed duct tape over her mouth and eyes and bound her hands and feet. She felt the van slowly drive away.

Eventually the vehicle stopped and she was carried from the van up some stairs and deposited in a chair. She felt her arms and legs being bound to the seat, and though she struggled, she quickly realized this was fruitless. She wanted to shout out her anger, but the duct tape was still in place and all she could do was mumble.

Finally, the tape was removed from her eyes and mouth.

"What the fuck...? Holy shit."

Her gaze was fixed on a table in front of her, where a long combat knife rested in a leather sheath. One of the Chinese men withdrew the blade and showed it to Cate. "Very sharp. Can cut very deep."

Her mind became filled with fear of what they were likely going to do with her. As she focused on the knife, she knew it would soon be used to torture her.

"What do you want? Don't hurt me. I'll pay you..."

The man in front of her was serious as he looked at her.

"You are hacker?"

"Yes, I'm a hacker." She reasoned that telling the truth might prevent these Asians from hurting her.

Why me? What have I done to you? Her mind turned to the various hacking attacks she had carried out and she visualized the people her hacking had affected. She could not recall any Asians who'd been hurt, but maybe they had been.

"You have control code which destroys computers. Yes?"

She realized that these men were looking for Mike, not her, and breathed a sigh of relief.

"No. That is not me. It's a friend of mine."

"Not true. It you."

"No. It's not me. I am a hacker, but that code—the delete code—was written by someone else."

"Who?"

She hesitated, knowing that if she told them about Mike, it would place him in severe peril. But the thought of being cut to pieces by these monsters filled her mind with horror.

"Okay. His name is Mike Young." She gave them his address. Her mind told her that her loyalty to a friend had not stood up in the least when she herself had felt threatened, but she reasoned that self-preservation was more important.

"I not believe you. You liar."

"No. I'm telling the truth. Go and ask him."

The man reverted to Chinese, a language that Cate recognized, and she assumed he was directing two others in his group to leave and kidnap Mike. She shuddered to think what they would do with him, but was happy that this would no doubt save her pain.

Then the Chinese man in front of her took the knife, and with a lightning-fast movement, sliced a long but shallow slash across her stomach. She screamed in pain.

"If you make lie, you suffer more."

While the Chinese held their brief interrogation of Cate, just a few streets away, the Chechen team had already located Mike Young having found Mike's address from the, now dead, Jeffrey Ayling. They entered the block of flats where the front door had been left ajar by someone lazy who did not want to use his key when returning from shopping. As they had acted in London for the assault on Atherton, two of the party of four took up positions at the front door to the building and the other two ascended to Mike's floor.

Finding his flat, they rang his doorbell.

Mike was writing code for his new video game at the time and hated to be disturbed. The game was his hobby, and he hoped shortly that he could devote most of his free time to it while sunning himself on his hundred-foot yacht in the Mediterranean.

"Wait. I'll be right there."

He finished a few lines of code he had thought through and then rose and went to the door. His mind was still on the code, and he opened the door without thinking or checking his peephole.

When he saw two Eastern-European-looking men dressed in suits, he asked, "What do you want?"

"Are you Mike Young?"

"Yes. Why?"

The first Chechen swung his hand around. It was holding a handgun, which was aimed at Mike.

"Inside."

The two Chechens entered his flat and looked around for anyone else present. Both had guns.

"Sit in chair." The order was clear, and with two armed men menacing him, Mike did so.

The second Chechen holstered his gun and withdrew a roll of duct tape, which he used to secure Mike's hands and upper body.

The Chechen leader called Kurbanova in Cyprus.

"Sir, we have captured the hacker. The man, Ayling, was braver than the man in London. It took a lot of torture to get him to talk. It was strange. At the end he kept saying 'single malt Scotch' over and over. Very odd, but he told us the name and address of the hacker."

"What did you do with Ayling?" Kurbanova asked.

"We killed him."

"Okay. Continue."

"We came to the address and I think we've found the hacker." The Chechen looked around the flat and focused his attention on the computers set up in the kitchen area. "We haven't interrogated him," he continued, "and I'm not sure that he is the hacker, but he has lots of computers and some are dead, as you expected. Shall we kill him?"

"Absolutely not. Do not harm him in any way. We have a customer who is interested in acquiring the man. An oligarch. Sanctioned. Needs money fast. He will pay well."

"Where do you want him delivered?"

"Take him to this address in Switzerland. Bundle up his computers—not the dead ones—and take them, too. I'll arrange a private jet from Leeds/Bradford airport to Zurich." He read out the address.

The leader expected the call to be terminated when his boss in Cyprus added, "Frederick, I have some bad news for you."

The leader wondered if he was about to be fired or swindled out of his fee.

"What, sir?"

"Your cousin, who was down in St. Vincent, has disappeared, along with his team. After the call which sent you and your men off to England, there was no communication, and his phone seems to be disconnected. I'll investigate, but I'm worried that the team has been arrested or worse."

"I understand."

The Chinese team left one man to guard the woman while the other five operatives approached the building where Mike's flat was located. They noticed two men overtly guarding the front door of the building.

The group leader said to his second-in-command, "He has guards. They must be his security detail. He must be the right man."

He signaled to his men and three scattered while he and the other moved down the street towards the front door of the building.

They chatted in Mandarin and advanced to the door, appearing to be residents returning home for the night. One of the Chechens stepped in front of them and said in accented English, "You cannot go. Closed for night."

Both Chinese men had dropped to a stoop, and in the darkness of the night, looked weak and harmless. One sidled back and close to the second guard and then the first drove a long knife into the throat of the man in front of him. The second Chinese man executed a similar move on the second guard, and other than rasping, guttural sounds, both men died quickly and quietly.

The Chinese group left one man on watch, but the other four entered the building and climbed the stairs to Mike's floor. They listened at the door and heard someone speaking Russian or some similar language on a telephone. None of them spoke Russian, so they could not understand the contents of the call, but it was obviously not a social interchange.

They waited until the call ended and then knocked on the door, having not seen the doorbell, and waited for a response. Their orders were specific: do not harm the hacker in any way, but their understanding was that the hacker was British and not Russian, or whatever language someone inside had been speaking. Perhaps they had the wrong address, or perhaps there were others involved. Then a gun fired from inside the flat and a bullet drilled through the flimsy door and caught the lead Chinese man in the chest. The others caught him as he fell and stood back out of sight from the peephole, which they now noticed.

The injured man grunted and slumped to the floor, but while he was hurt, the wound was not critical.

The second-in-command took charge and signaled the remaining two that they should prepare for a fire fight. He signaled to one of his men, who stepped forward, put a bullet through the lock, and kicked the door inward. The Chechens fired one or two more shots before being gunned down by the Chinese. None of the other Chinese operatives was hit.

Having ensured that the Chechens were both dead, they turned their attention to the British man restrained by the duct tape.

They removed the tape covering his mouth and he stared in disbelief at the two dead would-be kidnappers.

"You people got here just in time. I think they were going to kill me. Thanks so much."

The Chinese said nothing and Mike wondered who these rescuers were. They were not police, and that they were Chinese or some other Asian nationality seemed odd.

"Are you Michael Young?" one man asked.

Mike was about to verify his identity when he realized that although they had removed his mouth gag, they had made no attempt to release his hands and upper body.

"Who are you people?"

"Are you Michael Young?" One of them then slapped him hard across the face.

Mike cowered. "Yes."

"You are hacker? Yes?"

Mike hesitated and the man raised his hand again.

"Yes," he said.

The leader of the group, who had suffered the bullet wound, stood shakily and issued his orders in Mandarin.

"This is the hacker. Collect all the computers and bring him to the van. Administer the sedative. We'll pick up Wong and woman on the way and then head to the airport. Our next destination is Shanghai."

Chapter Fifteen

There were two private jets waiting at Leeds/Bradford airport. The one that had arrived first was chartered by a Cyprus bank, the second by a Chinese company.

The pilot and crew of the first had expected their passengers to arrive at the terminal within an hour of the plane's arrival, but that time had passed, and they observed the second jet load eight passengers and take off. After another half hour, the pilot made a call and was told to wait another hour before abandoning the flight.

Donna Strickland was frustrated. She had not had sex for several weeks, and now the trail to find the hacker had reached a dead end with the death of James Atherton. She was miserable and Jeff, who had joined her in her hotel room for a debrief, passed her a vodka from the minibar.

After taking a slug of the liquid from the small bottle, she put in a call to her boss's boss, Alan Harlan, using an encrypted voice application.

"Alan, I don't know what to do next. With Atherton dead, the case is shot. I have no idea who the hacker is or where he or she lives. There's no way I can see to pick up the lead." As she said this, her gaze rested on the TV in her room, on which a story was playing out. Jeff Acton was also watching it and snapped his fingers to get her attention.

"Alan, can you hold for a minute or two?"

Acton unmuted the television and watched the program, which was a Breaking News flash. It featured a torture/murder in London. The victim was identified as London financier James Atherton.

"Nothing new there," she said.

But then the newscaster announced another, similar crime in Bradford. This man was a local chief executive of a private company. The newscaster drew the obvious conclusion that these were linked, but then she reported another story set in Bradford about four Chechens, possibly linked to the Russian Mafia, being found dead in the flat of an independent programmer. The programmer was missing, and the police had requested help in contacting the man. The newscaster showed a photograph from a few years back, at university, and identified him as Mike Young.

The newscaster was handed another document and read it quickly.

"It seems that security cameras in the streets around the flat had been disabled and an investigation of this is also under way." She looked back up at the camera and continued, "We were allowed a quick look at the crime scene." Donna watched as the camera swept around the room. It picked up a white board at the top of which was written, 'delete code'.

"Gotcha" Donna said out loud.

She related the reports to Harlan.

"That's great, but who could have knocked out the team of Chechens?"

"I could have, but it wasn't me. Michael is in the U.S., so not him. Must be a third party and if this hacker, Mike Young, is missing, it sounds like a kidnaping."

In Cyprus, Kurbanova was angry. "Where the fuck are they?" The pilot of the chartered private jet had abandoned the flight when no one had shown up and the dispatcher had notified Kurbanova. His team in St. Vincent had disappeared, and now the team sent to Bradford had also broken off communications and not met the aircraft. Calls to them went unanswered. He was at his home outside of Nicosia and noticed a news program on his cable BBC channel that reported on the happenings in the United Kingdom. It was the first hard evidence he had that confirmed what he had suspected: the team had been killed.

First St. Vincent, and now in the UK. Who could be behind this?

The Chinese group decided to bring both Mike Young and Cate Glover with them, since they were unsure who the delete code hacker was. Possibly both were involved. They administered a powerful sedative to each and walked them on board the private jet, supported by the members of the group. They were strapped into their seats and secured by other restraints in the unlikely event that they regained full consciousness and became violent. During the flight, including the one stopover, one of the Chinese men administered more of the sedative to keep them in their docile state.

The plane flew into Shanghai Pudong International Airport and taxied to a remote area where several vehicles full of armed soldiers met them. A dozen soldiers moved to a semi-circle around the front of the plane, looking outward and providing a guard for the passengers. The Chinese team half carried Mike and Cate down the steps of the jet and then moved them to a waiting van. They were thrown into the back and secured to bolts in the vehicle. The team joined them and a soldier closed the door. Within another two minutes, they were speeding to a military facility that housed the Cyber Offensive wing of the Chinese military. At the facility, guards took over and moved the two hackers to a building and an elevator, which took them to the second floor. They were hustled down a short corridor, around a corner, and into a room with two single beds. Each prisoner was deposited into a bed and the guards withdrew, locking the door of the cell behind them.

It was late at night, and the guards knew that Dang Huan was at his home, sleeping peacefully, having been informed earlier that the hackers had been captured and were being flown across Eastern Europe and Asia to China.

The next morning, Dang Huan rose, bathed, and after his wife provided him his usual breakfast, he left his apartment and his driver took him to the offices where the two hackers were imprisoned. Before leaving for home the previous evening, he had arranged for an interrogator. With most of the world's computers and software being English-based, Dang and all of his hackers spoke excellent English, but Dang's skills did not extend to some of the more extreme methods of questioning.

Chapter Sixteen

On the plane trip to China, Mike had been sedated and unconscious most of the time, but when he awoke, he found himself in a small windowless room lying on a narrow single bed. His head ached and his mouth was dry with a metallic taste in it. On a bed opposite him lay another form. His curiosity aroused, he rose unsteadily and crossed the room. The other form was Cate Glover. *What the fuck is she doing here? For that matter, where the hell am I?* Then he remembered the Chinese men who had killed his Chechen captors in Bradford. At the time, for a few minutes he had thought they were going to save him. Then it became clear that they were to be his new captors. *What do these people want? It's probably the delete code, but it all seems heavy-handed for a set of ransomware code.*

Cate started to stir and he shook her awake.

"Cate, are you all right?"

She looked around and took in the cell.

"You fucker, Mike. You and your bloody code. What have you gotten us into?"

"Calm down. They'll probably let us go shortly." But he knew he was being foolishly optimistic.

The door opened and a tall Asian man in military uniform and insignia—showing he was of a senior officer—entered, followed by a soldier carrying a submachine gun.

"Oh, shit." It was clear they were in trouble.

"Welcome to Shanghai, Mr. Young and Ms. Glover," the Chinese officer said in good but accented English. Mike could tell the man was proud of his ability with the language.

"I am Colonel Dang Huan. My battalion of programmers is part of the Cyber Offensive group of the People's Republic of China."

The man was only a little older than Mike, perhaps in his early thirties, and to hold the rank of colonel probably meant that he was intelligent and an expert hacker as well as having sound military skills. Mike searched his memory for what he knew about the cyber battalions in the Chinese military and remembered that there were tens of thousands of programmers and hackers in China's employ.

What was obvious was that the Chinese were interested in Mike's code. Very interested, if they had killed a bunch of thugs in Bradford and shipped him and Cate over to the Chinese mainland. *Why Cate?* he wondered.

As his mind cleared, he had a wild thought. Perhaps they were not interested in his code as ransomware, but as a weapon to destroy computers. Perhaps all of those in the U.K. or more likely, all in the United States.

He asked the obvious question. "Why have you brought us here?"

"Don't be stupid, Mr. Young. We want what you call your delete code."

"Fat chance."

"I do not know that expression, Mr. Young. What do you mean?"

"I mean I'm not sharing it with you. I'm the only one who can send trigger codes, and I'm not doing it for a Chinese gig."

"What role does Ms. Glover have in your delete code?" Dang leaned forward.

Mike wanted to shield Cate and made the mistake of telling the truth.

"Nothing. She knows the code exists, but had no part in developing or testing it. She is just a friend."

Dang nodded. "As a friend, you will not want her to suffer, then."

"What do you mean?"

"We can be very cruel people, and I have a man here who delights in the pain of others. But I don't want to hurt you. I want you intact and able to operate your malware and show us how to use it."

The colonel paused and sat down on the bed where Mike had been sleeping.

"Ms. Glover is irrelevant to the code, so what we do with her doesn't matter. Does it? Let's go to another place that I call the interrogation room. We have nice chairs you can both sit in, and we shall continue this conversation."

The guard was joined by a second and they hustled Mike and Cate out the door of their cell and into a room close by. There was a stainless-steel table, and on each side chairs had been bolted to the polished concrete floor. Each of the chairs had attachments which would enable the occupant to be shackled and held securely. Mike looked around and shuddered. Cate whimpered. A guard pushed each of them into a chair opposite the other and the second guard stepped forward to secure their hands.

The first day was gentle, almost friendly. Dang used no force, but asked simple questions to test his prisoners' resolve and to establish their roles. He quickly reached the correct conclusion that while the woman knew about the code, it was the man who had written it and only he could control how it was used.

The second day of the interrogation was different. Cate was taken from their cell to the interrogation room alone. Dang Huan entered.

"Did they treat you well? Were you fed this morning?" His smile and his pretense of interest did not appear to impress the woman in front of him.

"Fuck off. What do you people want? I want to speak to the British consulate or embassy, or whatever."

Dang Huan laughed and they continued to banter for a few minutes. Then he stepped forward and slapped her hard across the face.

"Bring in the man."

A guard left and a minute later Mike was pushed into the room.

"Cate, did they hurt you?" Mike asked.

"A little."

But Dang saw that she thought, *Not badly...yet*.

The door opened again and a man bearing the rank of sergeant joined them. He wore a leather apron over his starched uniform. Dang smiled as the two guards, who each held semiautomatic weapons, cringed a little.

The Chinese man with the apron led the second day of interrogation.

His English was good, but not at the standard Dang had mastered. "Mr. Young, my colonel want you demonstrate how use this program of yours."

"Piss off."

The interrogator turned to Cate and glanced at a set of scalpels laid out in a leather holder on a nearby table. He hesitated about which to choose, but finally selected one with a short blade.

"Oh, shit," she said.

The sergeant proceeded to cut her t-shirt from her upper body. Then, as he looked at her faded bra, he slid the blade under her straps and removed it. She was now naked from the waist up, and she struggled to get free from her restraints. Mike also pulled at his, but they were secure. They both knew they were helpless and in the hands of a monster.

Dang viewed Cate's upper body and smiled. "Nice tattoos."

He turned his attention to Mike.

"You will do this for us, Mr. Young, or watch what pain we can inflict on your friend."

Dang saw that the male hacker was angry his friend had informed on him in Bradford, and that this had resulted in his capture by the Chinese. However, he believed that the hacker was weak and would try to protect his friend.

Mike shook his head.

"What do you want? Don't you Chinese have enough money from all the manufactured goods you ship into Europe and America?"

"I suspect, Mr. Young, that your code will allow us greater leverage than just extorting money from capitalists."

Dang could see that Mike understood the far more sinister aspects of his programming triumph.

"So, this is all about power. And you want to use the code against the West."

"You are a clever man, Mr. Young."

"Go to hell."

An hour later, Mike Young had just vomited. He was still in the interrogation room, shackled to his chair, but opposite him, Cate's naked body was a mass of blood where the interrogator had sliced into her. She had stopped screaming and had entered a catatonic state of shock from the pain and psychological effect of her body being shredded. She had pleaded with Mike to tell them everything to stop what they were doing to her.

"So, Mr. Young. Tell us the details of your malware. What is it? What can it do? Which computers have the code installed? How do we activate it?" Dang used a wet cloth to clean Mike's face and helped him drink from a glass of water.

Mike looked over at Cate. "Stop hurting her. I'll tell you everything."

Over the next hour, Mike conveyed most of the information about his code and how it was now installed worldwide. He described how it could be used to solicit ransom and the almost limitless amount of money it could yield. Dang asked questions and Mike answered them. The sergeant in the apron stood to the side and looked frustrated that he could not continue his onslaught on Cate's body.

In the corner of the room, one of the guards took particular notice of the dialogue and his eyes gleamed.

Dang Huan addressed the hacker. "Now, Mr. Young, time for you to give us a demonstration."

They moved the hacker to another room, in which his computers from Bradford had been set up. Cate was left helpless in her chair in the interrogation room, awake now and sobbing at the pain she had suffered. A medic treated her wounds superficially and then she was removed to another cell separate from the one she had shared with Mike.

Mike was seated in front of his main laptop and Dang said, "You will log in and then access what you have called your delete code dashboard. Think very carefully. If you do something to destroy the code or something else to damage it, you and your girlfriend will spend many painful weeks dying."

"She's not my girlfriend. She's just another programmer."

Dang Huan chuckled. "Who cares?"

Mike had been freed of his shackles and stared at the screen of his computer, trying to think of a way out of the situation. As he hesitated, the interrogator brought a scalpel sharply across his back, cutting deeply into his skin. He shouted out a curse.

Dang Huan glared at the interrogator. "Enough. You have done your job. Now leave us." The interrogator gave Dang Huan a slight bow and left the room. He paused in the corridor and then walked slowly back to the interrogation room.

"Do it, Mr. Young," Dang said. "Log on."

The little resistance Mike had developed a few minutes before dissipated and he leaned forward and logged in. For the next quarter of an hour, his fingers moved rapidly over the keys as he showed them how the dashboard was accessed and what functions he had built into the code. They instructed him to find the IP address and identifier of a computer in their facility and then issue the delete command. He did so, and as he hit the delete key on his dashboard, a battery of notification programs attacked the firewalls in the Cyber Offensive facility and finally succeeded in breaching the safeguards. The computer was stripped of its data, applications, and operating system. All the time, he was aware of blood oozing out of the wound on his back, and he resisted the urge to destroy the dashboard code.

"Show me how to use the system, Mr. Young."

"It's complex. Each time I log in, I need to use a different password, which I know how to do. Make one wrong move and it will self-destruct."

Mike knew that if he handed over all the protocols, his value would disappear and they would kill him.

"Tell me what you want it to do and I'll do it for you," he said.

Dang smiled. "Your approach is acceptable, Mr. Young. But remember what we can do to you and your friend if you change your mind."

Chapter Seventeen

The Bradford police had requested assistance from Scotland Yard, but both worked on the assumption that the murder of the Chechens was probably a local gang-related crime and focused on investigating gang members and their bosses within the Bradford area. They learned nothing.

The Purple Frog team knew, however, that the murder of the Chechens was part of something much bigger and conducted a wider search, including private jet departures from airports close to Bradford. One departure for Shanghai was the most likely exit path. They quickly discovered that the jet was owned by a Chinese company and further checks revealed its connection with the military in China.

One of the Purple Frog analysts briefed Harlan on their findings and he called Silvia into the meeting. "I reckon the bloody Chinese have kidnaped this Mike Young guy," he said, scratching his head. "This has to be much more serious than just a ransomware attack."

They both saw the potential threat immediately and called Ching Tong in.

"Damned Chinese," Ching said, and Harlan had to smile at the irony of the Chinese hacker's comment.

"How are your efforts going to remove this code?"

"Not good. We've burned through a dozen PCs, and every time we get close to accessing the code, it triggers the delete function. Fortunately, we kept those machines offline, since we found that the code also deletes backup files even if they're in the cloud. This programmer is very good."

Ching looked at some notes he had brought with him.

"There are a few dozen reports worldwide of computers that have suffered similar problems, so it looks like this malware could have been implanted on a wide range of systems. Perhaps every computer already has it installed. That's about two billion."

"Good God!" Harlan shook his head. "So, Ching, how do we stop it?"

"We have to just keep trying to find a way to remove it, or at least isolate the code. If we could find the hacker, I'm sure he'd be able to deactivate the malware. Oh, one thing we did find before one of the systems crashed was that it has some sort of filtering functionality. That probably means that our hacker can select which computers he deletes and which he doesn't. That's probably how he was able to demonstrate the reality of his threat to the bank in Cyprus. Don't know the details, but it's likely he uses the IP address of the router and perhaps the computer ID within the internal network."

Silvia had been somewhat skeptical about the importance of the malware but now recognized the power of the code. "So, he could wipe out all computers at a particular site?"

"Yes. And broader than that, all computers at a company or a government or even a country."

She stood and started pacing. "I wonder how much the Chinese know, and whether they see it as a way of making money or a way of destroying the West."

Harlan sat back. "With the efforts they have gone to, my guess is the latter."

Silvia Lewis sat down and said, "It's time I contacted Tina Graham."

After the analyst, Ching Tong, and Alan had left the meeting, Silvia placed a call to the CIA director.

"Tina, it's been a while."

"Yes. It has." The CIA director signaled for the officers, with whom she had been meeting, to leave her, and then continued the call. "This probably means there is a major threat that we at the CIA have not recognized. One that, somehow, you and your team have discovered. Am I right?"

"That's what I want to talk to you about."

Silvia explained Purple Frog's finding regarding the malware and that the hacker now seemed to be in the hands of the Chinese.

Tina listened and then groaned.

"If this delete code is as powerful as you say and it's in Chinese hands, it might be devastating."

Silvia heard Tina keying some notes into her computer.

Tina voiced her immediate plans. "The first thing I need to do is find out how broad the threat is. This malware might be very localized on just a few computers. Or, as you believe, it might be implanted on just about every computer worldwide. As soon as we find that out, I'll get the U.S. cyber people looking into it. If it's a major threat, I can have a thousand programmers working on it tomorrow, but before I mobilize the forces, I need to verify the scope. I can't believe our cyber people won't be able to solve the problem."

"From what we have found, it is prevalent. We have some very good hackers on our staff, but so far, they have been unsuccessful in being able to remove it. This is a tough one."

"Would one of our people be able to talk with your people?"

Silvia realized that she should have expected this, but had not thought through the implications.

"Probably. Let me think about it. Organize your test and I'll get back to you."

"I know the best person on my side to head this up."

The senior programmer Tina appointed to run the project held a Ph.D. in computer science and had a solid track record of tackling cyber warfare defenses. She quickly pulled a team together and they randomly tested computers across the world. Each one they tested triggered the code, destroying the resident data and backup. It was clear that the problem was broad in scope, and then, with Silvia's agreement, she spoke by phone with Ching Tong.

Later, Ching Tong reported to Silvia and Alan on their call. "The damn woman at the cyber intelligence group is so conceited. She has an ego bigger than a barn." Silvia and Alan exchanged smiles.

"The call was okay," he continued, "but she thinks that applying a thousand programmers to the problem will solve it. One thousand. That's crazy. You don't solve intellectual problems with brute force. Well, maybe in AI, but not with real humans."

Silvia cut off his rant. "Were you able to help?"

"A little. It's still too early to tell, but through our disciplined trial and error, we've learned a fair amount. The real problem is that as soon as we get close to understanding the problem, the code self-destructs."

He paused and took a sip of water from a Yeti bottle he always cared with him.

"I have six of us working on this, and the key seems to be rigorously documenting each step and each error as we make it so each can be avoided at the next round."

Harlan looked up from his notebook. "How many computers have we burned through?"

"A hundred and twenty."

"Bloody hell." Harlan did a mental calculation of the cost.

"I've also had one of our researchers looking into the upgrades. Based on the BigCat49 snippet, it looks likely that the hacker implanted the code through a normal software upgrade. The computers we've used in testing have minimal software, but are still infected, so it looks like it's either in the operating system or in one of the browsers."

"But those software companies have excellent anti-hacking staff to ensure piggybacking doesn't happen in their code."

"Well, this time, it looks like one crept through."

"And you told your girlfriend at the cyber intelligence group about your views on that as well?"

"Very funny. Yes, and she wrote it off as impossible. I reminded her of the Sherlock Holmes quote, 'When you have eliminated all which is impossible, then whatever remains, however improbable, must be the truth.' She laughed at me."

"So, you're not dating her?"

"God, no."

Chapter Eighteen

Alan Harlan arrived home at 7:00 p.m. that evening and Jess arrived a few minutes later.

"Alan, this bloody traffic is getting worse."

"It's always been terrible in the D.C. area, and the Beltway was never designed for this number of vehicles."

She tossed her keys into the bowl near their front door as Alan walked to the refrigerator and took out a bottle of Chardonnay, uncorked it, and poured a glass for his wife. He removed a single small ice cube and plonked it in a crystal whisky glass, then added an inch of his favorite single malt Scotch, Talisker Storm.

"Anything exciting at your secret agent organization today?"

"Actually, yes." He did not share most of the Purple Frog mysteries, but after their recent marriage and her help in solving the threat on the superyacht, *ECO-Ble*, he had been more forthright, and tonight he wanted to gather her expert opinion on the delete code.

"Do tell."

"We are in the early stages of what we see as a significant threat." He told her about the malware, how it was probably implanted in most of the world's computers, and the problems his hackers were having isolating it.

Jess nodded slowly. Since she worked for a defense contractor, her thoughts immediately went to the military uses that the delete code could be put to. "That is one helluva threat. This hacker could, potentially, wipe out all the data for a country's military, its government, a major competitor. You name it. You call it the 'delete code'?"

Alan swirled his Scotch in the glass. "Yes, and we need to find out how the code is triggered. We think it's already downloaded, but since we haven't heard of widespread computer failure, it must be waiting for some form of trigger. Maybe it's just on a timer, in which case the hacker needs to do nothing. More likely he'll send a simple code that triggers it. But how does he get that code through a company's firewall?"

"That's something I may be able to help with."

She finished her wine and motioned for Alan to refill her glass.

She continued, "In my work writing AI software, defense against cyber-attack is fundamental. All it takes is one person in the network to open a fake email and rogue code can be downloaded. In this case, the delete code is already in place and the trigger code is probably very simple and very hard to detect. It's probably able to sneak through the major antivirus software most people have installed."

He refilled her glass, and she took another sip.

"My bet is that your hacker has a bunch of phishing programs and message notifications, and any one of these can send a trigger for the code."

"But we still don't know how the code was piggybacked in."

Jess pulled her legs up onto the couch and said, "Probably a widget."

"A what?"

"A widget. There are stacks of routines which are common to all programs, and most software developers buy these and incorporate them in their code. They don't want to reinvent the wheel every time. They want to concentrate on stuff that drives their own application."

"For example?"

"You know when you click your mouse and move it over a string of text? It highlights the section of text and you can then cut, or copy and paste that somewhere else. I don't know for sure, but I expect some little software company wrote the machine code for that and that same code is used in every program that's out there. If they need to modify that code for a new version of the operating system, that company will issue an update and that will be included as part of everyone's next upgrade. Those small companies have rigorous anti-hacking protocols, but they don't have the same resources as a Microsoft or a Google." She sipped her Chardonnay and nodded. "Yes. I'll bet that was how it was done."

Alan sat back and laughed. "Tomorrow, darling, I am going to air my newfound knowledge about widgets and watch an egotistical programmer be amazed and likely pissed off."

"So, what's for dinner?"

Alan and Jess had continued their same separation of household duties after they had married. Alan had developed into a master cook and delighted in preparing and displaying meals that were above the ordinary. Jess, playing sommelier, chose a suitable wine from their increasing cellar and cleared up afterward. It had worked before the wedding and had done so since.

"Tonight, my darling, something different," he said.

"It often is, oh great chef."

He looked back and forth and was about to move his hands in a flourish when she put her hands on her hips.

"Alan, get on with it."

"It's Asian. A variation on poke bowl. Slices of raw yellowfin tuna, *cooked* in a dressing of soy, rice wine vinegar, sesame oil, garlic, and ginger."

"Cooked?"

"Actually, there is no heat involved. The cooking is achieved by the dressing acting as a marinade."

"So, the tuna is not cooked?"

"Not in the normal sense of cooked. No."

"Hmph."

"The tuna will be served over cold steamed coconut rice and with wakame."

"Wakame?"

"Seaweed salad."

"Sounds incredible, but a challenge for the poor little sommelier."

"I'm sure you'll cope."

He pulled her to him and kissed her.

"After I put the tuna in the marinade, we need to wait twenty minutes before it's ready."

"Oh. What'll we do while we wait?" She ran her fingers down his face.

"I have a great idea."

"Does the tuna need exactly twenty minutes?" she asked.

"No. Any time between fifteen minutes and an hour works."

"Perfect," she purred.

Chapter Nineteen

The sound of a smartphone's ring broke the silence and the Chinese woman in her apartment in Kuala Lumpur, Malaysia, reached over for it, saw the caller ID, and answered.

"This Betty Lau. Who you?" She spoke in English since the call was from Shanghai, and she knew that her contact spoke the foreign language, whereas many who might be listening in on the call did not.

"Miss Lau. This is Ling."

"Who Ling?" She knew the answer, but used this coded introduction to verify the contact was speaking freely and not under coercion.

"Ling is humble servant of Chinese state." He lied, but the answer coincided with the answer they had agreed on months before.

"I not know a Ling. Call someone else."

They hung up and a few minutes later, she sat at her computer with a headset on and took a call over an encrypted Telegraph channel from her contact in the Cyber Offensive group in the People's Republic of China.

"Ling, what you have for me?"

"Miss Lau, I not know if you accept this difficult feat, but prisoner in my organization has ability to demand huge ransoms from anywhere on planet."

Ling then spent the next twenty minutes explaining that, as a guard in the interrogation room, he had overheard the conversation during Mike Young's interrogation. He also told her of Dang Huan's interest in the code for military purposes.

"So, Chinese government want this hacker code for military attack? Yes? They not interested in stealing money?" Betty asked.

"Yes. That right."

"What waste."

"How is life in KL, boss?"

He used the common abbreviation for the Malaysian capital and Betty replied, "You not ask about my life, toad." She terminated the call and then sat in front of her computer, digesting what she had heard and thinking through the ramifications.

That evening she sat enjoying dinner with her lover, whom she knew as Bradly Johnson. She was aware, however, that this was not his real name.

"Brad, interesting talk with one of my men in China today."

"Oh? What about?" The man was Caucasian and spoke with a British accent. He was of medium height with an olive complexion. He looked up from his mee goreng at her words. His demeanor was one of confidence, but he did not stand out as an important or powerful man. Most people did not regard him as handsome, and those who met him could rarely remember much about him after their meeting. They usually failed to recognize him subsequently. For him, this trait was a positive rather than a negative. As one of the most formidable international assassins, being anonymous was a major plus.

Betty briefed him on her call with Ling and they discussed the value of what Betty described as the "kill code."

She saw that she had his attention.

"If we had this hacker, we get lots of money."

Brad laughed. "Are you suggesting we break this man out of a cell in the bowels of China's Cyber Offensive headquarters? That's madness."

"Perhaps. But if we could, there is big prize."

"It's insane, Betty. How would we do it? Would you go there and trade some batik for them to turn him over?"

"No, Brad dear. You go to Shanghai and rescue him. Bring him back here and we use code to make lot of money."

"Me? I'm an assassin. I'm not some action hero who fights his way into a jail guarded by the Chinese military and hidden somewhere in China. Do I then steal a jet fighter and fly back here? I don't have the skills. I don't even speak Mandarin. It would be suicide."

"Brad, dear. You have lot of skills, and I have gang in Shanghai which can help."

He put down his chopsticks, raised his glass of Carlsberg beer, and drank the quarter glass remaining.

"It's stupid," he said.

"It could mean we retire. Live on beach. Own big yacht. Have sex all day long."

Betty was drinking beer as well and rose quietly, went to the refrigerator, and brought back two more bottles.

He looked at her. She slid down on the seat next to him leaning forward, as she often did, revealing her cleavage and using it to get her way.

"That's a pipe dream," he said. "This is a mission impossible, and I'm not Tom Cruise."

"All right. Not easy, but why not try? Do you have project at moment? No. I'll set up with my gang and you meet them. If impossible, you come home, and we pass. If possible, think of the fun. The excitement. The big bucks."

He set his chopsticks down and sighed. "You have a point. This could be a big one. If we had this man and his code, we could collect big and neither of us would need to work again."

"Yes. Big risk, but big reward."

He rose from the dining table and walked to the windows of her high-rise apartment, looking out on the lights of Kuala Lumpur, which spread to the horizon.

"Each project I undertake brings in good money," he said, "but my real name is starting to leak out. More people than ever know of Abdul, the assassin. I have a lot of enemies out there, and if they knew where I was, they would use everything in their power to kill me. Revenge is a major human drive."

He returned to the table, sat, and shoveled some mee goreng into his mouth. After swallowing, he continued.

"As you know, I've been careful, and your skills in technology have helped keep me safe. Keep us both safe."

"Why not try break into Shanghai prison and kidnap hacker and his code? No need to steal Chinese jet fighter. I can arrange his move to KL and we get him work for us."

"You may be able to get him out of China, but getting him out of the Cyber Offensive facility is going to be impossible, as I've said. If he's as valuable as you say, they will have a heavy security force guarding him."

"Maybe so. Maybe not. Would you be into attempt get him out, Brad, dear?"

"It's not really my line of work. I'm not a jail breaker."

"But you have lot of right skills. Surveillance, stealth, ruthless, killing. These interchangeable."

"I don't speak Chinese, and I'll stick out like a sore thumb."

"You not look like sore thumb. You handsome."

"I mean that I am obviously Caucasian. Not Chinese."

"I have lots of assets in Shanghai. They help."

Brad knew about her links to a criminal gang based in Shanghai. Betty's father had led the gang until he was killed by rivals and Betty had taken over and carried out her retaliation. The organization worked independently, but paid part of its profits to

Betty as its titular head. The gang also helped her out when violence was a part of her strategy to grow her batik empire.

Brad laid down his chopsticks. "I'll need a team to pull this off."

"I have fifty men with different skills: theft, burglary, murder, interrogation... You name, Brad. I got."

"Can you get plans for the facility?"

"I not stupid. I have already. Here." She reached behind her and took a sheath of papers from a nearby coffee table. She handed him a scanned hand-drawn plan for each floor of the facility.

"The crosses show each guard. On duty most of time."

"Not as many as I would expect."

"Ling says not many know about value of this *laowai*. Everyone keep very secret."

"So, I'll fly to Shanghai, meet your gang, spring this hacker from his prison, and bring him back to KL. Is that what you want?"

"Brad, dear, I knew I love you. Feel like sex? Sex so good."

Brad Johnson had been living in the Malaysian capital for two years, and while he and Betty Lau did not live together, they spent every night with each other in either his apartment or hers, except when one of them was away on business. Betty had her batik empire, which had expanded throughout the Far East, and Brad spent time researching, planning, and then assassinating individuals across the world.

If he could pull this off, the money they could acquire would enable him to give up his trade and retire with Betty. He liked the idea, and although he was concerned about the practicality of the mission, he nodded his acceptance.

"Let me make the arrangements."

"Already done, Brad dear. You need tidy up things so leave in one week. Flight already booked. This exciting, Brad. You know what Betty wants when excited. I want sex. Now."

Chapter Twenty

Doris, Jason's housekeeper in their home in St. Croix, brought a cup of tea to Sarah as she lay on an outside bed by the pool. She looked down at the frail woman and held back a tear. Sarah had become weaker in the last few weeks, and everyone knew that the end was near. Jason had brought a specialist doctor down to the island with them, and he prescribed increasing levels of painkillers, which softened the effect of the growing cancer. However, they made her continually tired and she spent most of her time sleeping. She had been clear with Jason that since her condition was terminal, she did not want to use any invasive treatments, and the specialist had agreed with her decision.

When she was awake, she was anxious to take advantage of her remaining days. She talked incessantly about her life with Jason, the birth and growing up of their two daughters, and the raft of achievements in her life. Jason allowed her to drive the conversation, which focused on several episodes of their life together.

On one occasion, they had taken a large, twin motor catamaran out in the British Virgin Islands and had nearly been wrecked when both engines had cut out in the middle of a storm and their craft had been swept towards rocks in the Sir Francis Drake Channel. The problem had been faulty fuel, but Sarah and Jason's actions and rescue by a passing boat had saved them. They had talked about this adventure many times, and had always laughed at the humor of a technology billionaire almost crashing on the rocks. Sarah brought up the incident again and they roared with laughter until her contortions added to her pain and she collapsed, exhausted, on the bed.

Jason tried to keep busy, but having resigned as CEO of Avanch, he found he had a lot of time on his hands and little to occupy him. When Sarah was sleeping, he spent some time with her, but had periods when he took breaks and needed to find something to do. For all his life, he had worked hard, logging long hours to build and sustain his company. Now, he wandered around his estate and read books and newspapers when he was not sitting with the woman he had loved for so many years.

He had decided that he would stay out of Avanch's business unless the new CEO called him with questions or to seek his advice. This happened less than he'd expected, and he took this to be a positive sign that he had groomed the man well. However, he felt pangs of annoyance that the company seemed to be able to function well without his talents and experience. He did not appear to be missed at all.

He was still on the board of Avanch, and also had a number of outside directorships, but these took little time, so he redirected his activities to Purple Frog and had been briefed on the delete code threat.

He spoke with Silvia by phone about the issue. "So we think that the British hacker is in China?" he asked.

"Yes. We traced the aircraft to Shanghai, but after that, we have no idea where he was taken. We know the aircraft is owned by a shell company, which is owned by the Chinese military, so we can assume that they may want to use his code as a potential weapon."

"If what you have described is right, this threat sounds formidable. Can we get the hacker out? Doesn't the CIA have agents over there who can rescue him?"

"Tina seemed unhappy going down that path," Silvia said. "The U.S. and China relations are at a new low, and she doesn't want discovery of what the Chinese will, no doubt, call a CIA plot. She thinks the

NSA cyber intelligence group will be able to isolate or remove the code and the threat will just go away."

"Any progress on that?"

"No. The U.S. has about one thousand programmers working on the code, and has also involved the main software companies, including Avanch, so they should be able to solve the problem. Let's hope that's the case."

Jason was sitting in his office under Sugar Ridge and wrote a few notes on a yellow pad. "As a plan B, though, why doesn't Purple Frog take another path and see if we can rescue this Mike Young guy before he passes over all his secrets?"

"If he hasn't already done so."

Jason wrote three exclamation marks next to where he had written "Get hacker out."

"Right, if he hasn't already done so," he agreed. "But even if he has, getting him into U.S. hands should level the playing field."

"I've already got Alan working with Michael on a plan."

"Good. I'm going to reach out to Henry Ju-long. He and his wife were cleared of charges in China and have returned there. He's in commercial real estate and might have some contacts to help us identify where Young is being held." Jason had already written Henry's name on his pad.

After the call with Silvia, he called the Chinese ex-billionaire on an encrypted line they had established years previously and they spent a few minutes in personal discussion—Sarah's progress, or lack of it, and how Henry's wife, May, was reacting to her return to China.

Henry then said, "As much as I like talking with you Jason, you probably have a specific reason for calling..."

"You're right, as always."

Jason told Henry about the delete code and his fears that China could use it against the U.S. or other countries.

"This serious stuff," Henry said. "President Yang has shown signs of burning global ambition lately. A few years back, he directed attention to building his power base in China. Rivals arrested and imprisoned, and dissenters crushed without mercy. He consolidated his power inside China and has now switched to ambitions outside the country. The delete code might be a significant play for him. What are you planning?"

"Best you don't know, old friend."

"How can I help?"

"I don't want to place you in any peril, but we need to find out where Young is being held, and preferably get some floor plans of the facility. Plus, the security there. Anything you can get"

"You mentioned this is probably in Shanghai. With emphasis on cyber warfare, this is probably a play by the Cyber Offensive organization. They have a headquarters building in Jinshan, just outside Shanghai. Let me see what more I can find out and call you back."

"Henry, don't put yourself at risk. Be very careful."

"I will." He hung up.

Four hours later—and Jason noted that it was 2:00 a.m. in China—Henry called back.

"My people tell me there has been increased activity at the Cyber Offensive facility in the last week. Not a lot, but more than before, and security is tighter. Good guess that is the place. My firm has copies of architectural drawings of all buildings in the area, and I am sending you a copy. I can't risk exploring further, but this gives you a starting point. Stavros and I own a building close by, so please don't send in a badly guided missile to destroy the Cyber Offensive facility. It could hit me." Henry chuckled.

Jason received the plans a short time later and forwarded them to Silvia. She called him back.

"Jason, I received the plans. They're useful, but don't tell us much. At least we have an address and a general layout so Michael and his merry men will have a starting point."

"Don't let Donna Strickland hear you calling them 'merry men.' You'll have a sexual harassment suit on your hands." They both laughed and Jason hung up.

Chapter Twenty-One

Having broken Mike's resolve, Dang Huan worked with the British hacker to understand the intricacies of the delete code, how it could be triggered, and the booby-traps it contained to prevent its removal. On a couple of occasions, he was outraged when Mike refused to provide specific answers to his questions, but a visit to the interrogation room to see his programmer friend, who was also brought in, quickly persuaded the hacker to change his mind. On one occasion, Dang noticed that his interrogator was abusing Cate without reason and ordered him to cease.

Dang now had most of what he wanted, so the colonel presented details of the code and a strategy for a major attack on the United States to the governing board of the Cyber Offensive group. They questioned him for an hour, and he easily fielded their queries and had Mike provide a demonstration of the code. The board was delighted at the simplicity of this approach and its incredible power as a weapon.

A senior member of the board, an older man in his seventies, raised an issue which reflected his lack of understanding of the role of computing in today's world.

"So, Dang. Your little toy wipes out the computers. But Americans can still send their war ships and tanks and airplanes and troops. How does killing computers help?"

Dang kept his frustration in check and replied, "You're right, General. If we destroy all of the American army's normal computers, their weaponry and their troops remain intact. But, we shall have destroyed their ability to use them. The code will destroy all their personnel records, all their inventory records, their supply chain data, their payroll, their scheduling, and most of their communications."

The governing board started to understand.

Dang continued, "They won't know what weapons and ammunition they have in stock. They won't be able to ship them to the front line, wherever that is. They won't know what troops are where, nor be able to redeploy them. They won't know when to re-order ammunition. The army will not be able to pay their soldiers and their generals, and when the troops are not paid, they will revolt. It won't destroy the soldiers and the weaponry, but it will make them impossible to use."

The board signaled their appreciation for the presentation and Dang's insight. He was instructed to make the same presentation to others in the chain of command, and over the next week he did so, finally reaching the office of the president.

President Yang, commander in chief of the People's Republic of China's military forces, sat at a long table in his palace overlooking the Forbidden City in Beijing.

Dang Huan made his presentation and Yang quizzed him for an hour, then demanded a demonstration. Dang had expected this and had a computer brought into the meeting room. A security guard examined the system closely to ensure there were no weapons or bombs hidden in it and nodded to the president.

Dang logged on to this computer and navigated to a display of a standard Chinese browser window. He called his operations center and instructed Mike to access the computer and delete its contents. A few minutes later, he did so, and the computer screen went dark. A senior IT specialist on Yang's staff was present and examined the computer. He attempted to restore it without success and stated that the delete code had functioned as Dang had described.

"So, tell me, Dang Huan: How can this be used?" The president was impressed, but a little skeptical.

"We can destroy all of America's computers. Their industry will remain intact, and there will be few, if any, civilian or military casualties. It does not cost anything, and we can accomplish the victory in a matter of minutes."

"America is still our largest export market by far, and if their economy collapses, no one will buy from us."

"True, sir, but we can target specific sectors or groups of people, just as I singled out that computer over there and not all of China's computers."

Yang walked back and forth as he thought about the use he could put the code to. "We could destroy their computers, Dang. But perhaps more powerful is just the threat of doing so."

His mind visualized the power of the malware. What had Dang Huan called it? The delete code.

With tens of thousands of hackers in the Chinese military, none had been able to rival the destructive power this weapon held. They had built malware that would disable power utilities across the U.S. or in other enemy countries. This was ready to be made operational, but they had nothing as powerful as the code that this single British programmer had created.

A plan for its first deployment came into his thoughts and his strategic mind quickly formulated a series of follow-up operations, which would result in world domination for China.

"Dang Huan, good work. But before my first move, I must be sure that the code will work. Thorough testing must be undertaken immediately. I want it completed within a week. Go."

The National Security Agency's cyber intelligence group had started their analysis of the code threat several weeks before Dang's presentation to Yang. They were briefed by their management about the likelihood of malware being implanted in a wide range of computers and that it could provide a major threat. After initial scoping confirmed that the threat was widespread, a team of nearly a thousand programmers was assembled to locate and remove the code. The first step was to locate where, on each computer, the phantom code was hiding. The senior programmer in charge of this large force had been instructed to speak with a mysterious outside contractor who had been found by the CIA and had views on the malware. When she'd spoken with him, he'd used voice modification software, adding to the intrigue. He had been adamant that throwing large numbers of programmers at the problem would not provide the result they were seeking, but she'd scoffed at his views.

Some bloody contract hacker, she thought. Now, she was starting to believe the man. Her team, now in excess of eleven hundred programmers, had worked diligently, but had also accidentally activated the code and destroyed over four thousand computers without coming any closer to locating and deactivating what was known as the delete code.

They had also reached out to the major software companies confidentially, and these bastions of technology had also failed.

With an official order from President Yang, Dang Huan returned triumphantly from Beijing and started the implementation of the plan. He met with Young and told him the first steps.

"We must be sure the system will work. We will test it on computers in China and outside. Testing must be complete in five days."

As he worked on the testing stage, Mike was in a miserable state. He did not yet know the target Dang Huan would provide him, but he was sure it would be substantial and impact one or more Western countries. He struggled back and forth with the ethics of doing what was demanded, but knew that they would continue to torture Cate in front of him, and probably start on him next.

He had convinced them that only he could negotiate the dashboard and select targets, so they did not have a way of activating the code without him. He signaled to a guard that the testing was complete and was ordered to stand aside while Dang and another programmer checked the results.

"Mr. Young, congratulations. Testing shows that your code is everything you have told us it is. A week ago, I met with the president, and he gave me his orders for next stage. You and I will make an historic attack on the United States government."

"I'm not going to do it," Mike told the colonel.

Dang slapped him and called out some orders. A few minutes later, Mike was dragged into the interrogation room and Cate was brought in. She was still naked from the waist up, and while some of the initial cuts had healed, others showed signs of infection, and she was screaming with the knowledge of what would happen next.

The sergeant, again wearing his leather apron, entered the room and smiled at the scared woman.

She was forced to sit again and shackled into her chair opposite Mike.

Mike broke. "Stop. Okay. I'll do what you want."

Dang had the guards free Mike and then escort him to the computer room. The colonel stayed behind for a minute or two, looking at Cate's wounds and recognizing the sadistic tendencies in his sergeant.

"Have your fun, sergeant, but she must not die. She might be needed later," he said in Mandarin, and then he joined the others, leaving Cate and the interrogator alone together.

The sergeant watched his boss leave and then turned to face Cate. His colonel had instructed that she must not die, but had not said not to cause her more pain. He sniggered and reached for a scalpel he was particularly fond of. He also eyed a simple hammer. Her screams were deadened by the sound proofing in the room.

The next week, the chief of staff in the White House was sitting in front of his computer screen when it went blank.

"I must have knocked the plug out," he said to himself as he crawled under his desk. The plug was still attached to the power outlet, so he scratched his head and tried to reboot the system. This did not work, so he put in a call to his regular IT support person, a young woman whose figure the chief of staff lusted over. He could not help focusing on her body as she crawled under his desk. She checked out the system, but could not identify the source of the mystery.

"Don't know what the problem is. I'll get you a new system while we check it out." She did so and loaded the new computer with all the needed software and file access. A few hours later, that computer, too, went dark. The support person talked with her manager, who diagnosed the problem as potential malware, and as a matter of protocol, called the FBI. A special agent there referred him to the cyber intelligence people in the NSA, and a senior official in that agency recognized the issue and explained the threat they were facing. The chief of staff called an emergency meeting and was thoroughly briefed on the delete code and the futile efforts to date of attempts to eliminate it.

Another day passed and the president of the People's Republic of China placed a call to the president of the United States. There had not been this level of communication for a year as relations between the two superpowers had deteriorated.

The Chinese president came straight to the point.

"Mr. President, I want to alert you that we shall be moving a large military force to our islands in the South China Sea as a proactive role against imperialism by the United States and other countries in that region. As you well know, these are Chinese waters."

"President Yang, that would be unwise. They are not Chinese waters, and you know we wouldn't allow that move without responding with a major intervention."

Yang replied, "I demand your defense forces stand down, and you must instruct your allies in the region to do the same."

"And if I don't?"

"There is something you may have heard of. The delete code. Ask your chief of staff about that."

The president's chief of staff was party to the meeting, and he had briefed the president about the malware just an hour before the call.

The president had always prided himself on keeping calm and non-committal in the most turbulent of times, and said, "Yes. I have heard of it. So what?"

"With one keystroke, we can destroy all your government computers and the data associated with them. Your backups will also be destroyed. Your administration and all the government departments across the U.S. will be eliminated. No deaths or injuries, but your power will be gone. You will face turmoil."

The U.S. president closed his eyes at the thought of this attack.

Yang continued, "Please spend the next week deciding about the South China Sea. You hold off your forces and we occupy the whole set of islands. The alternative is you lose all your computer power. No payroll, no tax records, no military and intelligence files, no supply chain management. We'll start with the CIA."

Chapter Twenty-Two

After the call, the president called his national security team to a meeting in the Situation Room to decide what actions they could take.

The president started. "This threat seems real. Tina, how do we stop it?"

Tina Graham reported on the current investigation that the NSA's cyber intelligence group was conducting, but had to tell him that, to date, they had been unable to find a way to deactivate the malware. She filled him in on more details about the British hacker.

"This Mike Young. Where is he?" the president asked.

Tina replied, "We believe he's in China. He was kidnapped from the U.K. and flown to Shanghai, but just where in that city, we don't know."

"Damn it, Tina. Have your spies over there find out."

"Our coverage has never been as good there as in other countries, but we do have them all looking."

"How do we know that this isn't just a bluff?"

The chief of staff answered before Tina could. "Well, Mr. President, our IT staff hasn't been able to explain what happened to my two computers yesterday, but all my data and programs are gone. I believe this threat is real."

The president moaned. "And this is just the beginning. This is the thin end of the wedge. The stakes in the South China Sea are relatively small, but if we give in to Yang on this, he'll come back for more later. I bet I know what that'll be."

He sat back.

"The PLA already have plans to invade Taiwan, and if they can blackmail us into not intervening, it'll be a cake walk for them."

The chairman of the Joint Chiefs of Staff responded to the president, "Not necessarily. The Taiwanese have built their military force dramatically over the past few years, and the population is adamant about not being taken over by mainland China. We thought that Ukraine would be a pushover for the Russians and were wrong on that."

"But," the president interjected, "the Taiwanese think they can depend on us to support them. That has always been our position, so if we don't, God knows what will happen. And the Chinese will likely use this delete code on Taiwan. This is a damn mess."

The secretary of defense then added, "Bottom line is that we have to neutralize this malware offensive."

The president pounded the table in front of him. "People, get on this now. Find me a solution. We only have seven days, so move it."

As the meeting was breaking up, Jim Solomon, the director of the NSA and Tina's boss, pulled her to one side.

"Can your clandestine friends help with this?"

"They're the ones who alerted me to the situation in the first place."

"Perhaps we should close the CIA and subcontract everything to this group. You called it 'Well-wisher,' didn't you?"

Tina was fairly sure he was joking. But not entirely so.

One aspect of the U.S. political scene is the extraordinary number of information leaks even relating to the most secret of matters. In this case, within an hour, a summary of the call between the U.S. president and Yang found its way to a member of

Russia's embassy in Washington, who had the official title of assistant secretary for cultural affairs. In fact, he was a member of the FSB, with his primary duties in espionage.

He spent a little time confirming the efficacy of the Chinese threat, then passed the details to his bosses in Moscow. Within a day, the Russian president, Dimitri Chekhov, had been informed and called his head of cyber security into his office.

"Colonel Snarof, the Chinese have some cyber weapon and say it can remove all data from the CIA's computers. They are using this malware as a threat."

"Doesn't sound plausible to me, sir."

"Why not?"

"They would have to have some code downloaded into the CIA computers, and that is almost impossible. Their firewalls are much too good. We've been trying for years and getting nowhere."

"My source says the American president is taking it seriously. Something about a demonstration that the Chinese pulled."

The colonel gave a slight nod of his head. "That's different. If they were able to demonstrate it, perhaps they have something."

"Colonel, how can they have this and you don't?"

"We have thousands of programmers working on cyber defensive and offensive strategies, but the Chinese have several times the number. Brute force? Maybe they were just lucky. Maybe I need a larger headcount."

"Do you have spies in the Chinese hacker groups?"

"Of course. A hundred or so, but they're scared to communicate anything really important. We only receive minor pieces of information. If this malware really exists, the Chinese will be safeguarding it well, so it's unlikely I'll be able to find out anything, but I'll check it out."

The Russian president was furious. "You're useless. Get out."

Chekhov thought about the matter for an hour and consulted several of his aides and advisors. They all reached the same conclusion. The hold the Chinese seemed to have over Washington seemed real, and Russia had not been included in the dialogue.

Finally, Chekhov had his staff place a call to his Chinese counterpart.

Within a half hour, the two presidents spoke over a secure line.

"President Yang. It's been many weeks since we last spoke. How are you?"

Yang hated small talk and answered curtly, "Dimitri, you didn't call to ask about my health." The Chinese simultaneous translator attempted to soften the message, but was unsuccessful.

The Russian spoke with some hesitation. "Our people tell me you have a new weapon that you are planning to use against the Americans. Is that true?"

"What if it is?"

"We have a partnership. We look after each other. We support each other."

"Rubbish. What have you done for me?"

"President Yang, Russia supplies you with oil and gas. Our prices are special for you. Well below what we charge others. We support you all the time in the media."

"Hmph."

"On a personal level, I have made significant funds available as part of our friendship. I have even provided you with a superyacht in the Pacific."

"Stop the bullshit. What do you want?"

"Since we are partners in our fight against the West, can we not share your clever little malware code or whatever it is?"

"No. You have shown your stupidity with your actions in Ukraine. What you took to be an easy operation has bogged down and you have lost half of your military resources. And other European states are now joining the EU and even NATO."

Chekhov bristled but Yang continued.

"You have shown poor decision-making. If we were to share the delete code with you, who knows what idiocy you would pull next? You might decide to wipe out Germany on a whim."

Yang's anger was increasing, and the interpreter was feeling the brunt of Chekhov's fury, which was also rising.

Yang continued, "What we have is the greatest weapon ever invented, and we are not sharing. In fact, Mr. President, I can see a day when we might want to use it against Russia. Perhaps your oil prices are too high, and we shall use the code in the renegotiation."

Yang hung up.

Chekhov looked out his office window at the gray streets of Moscow covered by a thin line of snow. Then he threw his phone at the wall of his spacious office.

Chapter Twenty-Three

In their initial interchanges, Silvia had always initiated calls with the CIA Director but recently she had provided Tina with a telephone number which passed through a series of links and safeguarded the Purple Frog location.

Tina called her and Silvia picked up.

"Hi, it's Tina."

"Hi." Silvia answered.

Tina told her about the threat from the Chinese president.

"Holy shit."

Silvia thought about what Tina had told her. She already had a team, including the profiler who was dedicated to researching Yang, work up several scenarios, and one described the Chinese president using the code as a threat to gain political advantage. She had not thought it would manifest itself so quickly.

"What is the president going to decide?"

"He's adamant that he'll not give in, but the impact of the attack—if it comes and does what Yang says—is huge. To lose all the data in the CIA would be devastating."

"How are you going to react?"

"We've already backed up a lot of our files to other networks, but there are security risks, and we won't be able to mirror every computer we have. On the record, we have twenty-three thousand employees, but the real number is a lot higher. And most of those are spread all around the world."

"What about the source? Can you rescue the hacker?"

"My initial thought as well. Logically, we would use a squad in China to find the hacker and either rescue him, or, frankly, eliminate the threat."

Silvia had played with these options as well, but decided to challenge the CIA director.

"Eliminate? You'd just kill him?"

"Preferably not, but if that's the only option, we'll do what we have to do."

Silvia had a cup of coffee in front of her and took a sip.

Tina continued, "But we don't have many resources on the ground there, and we only have a week. Yang has already instigated a round up of many of our agents, and we face this ticking time bomb."

"Send in a squad from here, or Japan?"

"We can't be seen sending in a hit squad. The president made that very clear."

"So, what did he suggest?"

"He suggested that the CIA find a way to solve his problem."

"So, you are asking for help from Well-wisher?"

The CIA director sighed. "Yes. Yet again."

Silvia drained her cup. "What did you have in mind?"

"Can you terminate the hacker or, better still, get him out? Do you have resources in China?"

"No, but we might have an approach." Silvia paused and then added, "Chances are he has already passed over all the information about the code. What it does, how to access it, and how to trigger it. If we eliminate him and that is the case, it won't solve our problem."

"You're right. The best scenario is that we get the hacker out. Bring him to U.S. soil. He's sure to have a way to remove the code and nullify the threat. And if we can leave China's computers with the malware in place, we will have one helluva bargaining chip."

"We don't have much time. Operations like this need planning."

"I know. But we don't have more time."

"Tina, let's say we agree and, against all odds, are successful. What happens to the hacker?"

"He and his code will become a property of the United States. It's your country as well as mine, I'm guessing." Tina did not know Silvia's nationality nor location, and her voice had always been distorted by a software voice modifier, but from Purple Frog's actions in the past, the CIA director surmised that Well-wisher was American.

"And will you use this delete code against China?"

Tina was silent and then spoke. "It's possible. We might just use it as a deterrent."

"Not very convincing." Silvia hesitated. "I'll tell you what. We don't have much time, so we'll try for the rescue. If we're successful, we'll need a safe house in the U.S. for him. We'll keep him there for a week while we discuss terms. Are you okay with that?"

"I don't like it, but I have no other choice. I'll set up the safe house. Where do you want it?"

"LA."

When she hung up with Tina Graham, Silvia called a meeting with Michael McKnight and Alan Harlan.

Michael guessed the subject and gathered up some papers, which he took to the meeting.

Silvia started before the African American had even taken his seat.

"Michael, I know you've developed preliminary plans for a rescue attempt, but the timescale has changed. What are the odds of doing it in the next week?"

"Honestly, Silvia?"

"Yes. It sounds impossible, but the fate of the U.S. is hanging on either getting this Mike Young character out, or, I guess, eliminating him and destroying his triggering code."

She gave the two men details of her call with Tina and the threat which now hung over the United States.

McKnight shook his head. "We think we know where he's being held. But there are a lot of things we don't know. What security do they have? Do they expect an attack? And, for that matter, do we know that he's not just partnering with them? It may not have been a kidnap at all."

"I agree. There's a lot we don't know."

"Silvia, we need more time to plan this. By the time we arrive in Shanghai, we'll only have about five days before the president's deadline is up. A mission like this needs much more time to get it right. It could be suicide."

"I'm sorry, Michael. I can't give you more time. Is the exit plan in place?"

"Yes. The ship can be in Shanghai within that timeframe."

Silvia stood and paced the conference room. Everyone knew this little foible and waited without speaking for her to reach a decision.

"Michael, take your team and go to China. Do what you can. Don't sacrifice the team, and if you can't pull it off in time, we'll live with that. I'll organize a jet from Jason to get you there."

"What if we can't get him out?"

"Ching Tong believes that the hacker is the key. If you can't rescue him, terminate him and destroy whatever computers he seems to be using."

McKnight had seen Silvia Lewis change over the past several years. She had been repulsed by physical violence and reluctant to authorize it. Killing was always a major problem. Now, she had accepted that termination was a satisfactory approach if there was no other option.

He continued. "We'll need to take some equipment with us. Using Jason's private jet will save us a day or so. I'll think through what we need to take and brief the team this afternoon. I'll take Donna, Paul, and Tom. More than four will be way too obvious." He stroked his short beard and continued. "Do we need an Advisory Board okay?"

Harlan answered, "Yes, as always." McKnight hated paperwork, particularly that which was required for Advisory Board approval of a mission.

"Don't worry, Michael," Harlan said. "I'll attend to all that."

McKnight left the meeting and went directly to David Osler's office. McKnight had renamed Osler "Q" after the James Bond character. The tall man provided all the armaments and other "toys" for their various operations.

McKnight outlined the mission, explaining they would be taking Overly's jet, which had a special, secret compartment so they could arrive in Shanghai with whatever armaments suited the situation.

Osler was pragmatic and direct. "I'll let you all have Glock 9mm handguns, combat knives, and P90 submachine guns."

"Good. The P90s are Belgium from FN, right?"

"Yes."

"That's the 9mm parabellum version, right?"

"Yes. I'll provide five magazines already loaded for each, as well as a lot of extra ammo. The bullets are the same for both the SMGs and the Glocks."

"Efficient as always."

McKnight assembled his Purple Frog field operations team at the Purple Frog office in northern Virginia, and they were driven to Dulles International. Late that afternoon, they boarded the private jet and buckled in. The pilot called for clearance to take off and a few minutes later they gained speed down the main runway and left the ground, turning in a westerly direction on the flight to Shanghai.

Chapter Twenty-Four

A day later, Abdul—using his Bradly Johnson passport—flew to Shanghai, but on arrival at the Chinese city, he offered a different passport in the name of William Lamb, a citizen of the United Kingdom, to the immigration officer.

"Why you come to Shanghai, Mr. Lamb?" The Chinese official was polite but suspicious.

"To see the wonderful sights of your city and eat the best cooking that China has to offer." He laughed and the immigration officer stamped his passport and welcomed him.

Abdul took a taxi to the hotel where he was registered. He checked his room for bugs, found none, and made a call on his mobile phone.

"This is Yee," his contact answered.

They arranged to meet in Abdul's hotel room, and an hour later a short but muscular Chinese man knocked on his door and Abdul ushered him in.

Yee spoke passable English, and since Abdul did not speak Mandarin or any of the local dialects, this was their only way of communicating.

Yee looked at the assassin. "Miss Lau has instruct me give all help you need. I am head man of gang. I can get many men if you need."

"Okay. Do you have any contacts in the Cyber Offensive facility?"

"Just Ling, and he is talk man, not action."

"So how do we break in?"

"Very difficult."

Just over a mile away, another team was planning a similar operation. Michael McKnight and his team had arrived in Shanghai the day before, and had already driven past the site of the Cyber Offensive operation. Henry Ju-long's plans of the facility were exact, but he had not been able to provide details of the security measures, which left a gap in Purple Frog's intelligence.

McKnight had little time for preparation, knowing they would need to rescue or kill Mike Young before the one week deadline expired. An armed attack would be fruitless since even if his team was successful, back-up forces would be called in from the Chinese military and escape would be impossible.

"We need to infiltrate the complex in some way and remove Young without raising a hornet's nest," McKnight said.

Tom Harness, a newer member of the team and an Australian, came up with the idea which seemed most likely to succeed.

"Well, mate, the facility is a computer hub, so it must have a shitload of electric power going in there. Let's take that out and it'll kill the lights and any security cameras at the same time."

Strickland leaned her head to one side and countered, "But they're sure to have back-up generators and UPS—uninterruptible power supplies—so they'll only be out for milliseconds."

"Right on, Donna, but they'll need to have someone from the power company or whatever China has to diagnose and fix the problem. If we can intercept them and take their place, we should get in easy." Australians were usually pragmatic.

McKnight pondered the approach. "It might work. Since there won't be any real power interruption, only the maintenance staff will notice. They'll regard it as a routine problem and an easy fix by the power company."

"One problem, Michael." Donna was also a pragmatist. "The power technicians will be Chinese, and that we are not."

"Let's go and check out the complex again. It may give us some inspiration."

That night, they moved quietly up a small knoll about a half mile from the Cyber Offensive facility. They had left their P90s behind, but each carried a 9mm Glock. There were five buildings in the facility, and the plans that Henry had provided indicated that the central one was the most likely to be the location of the hacker. The complex was outside the main city and surrounded by barren, empty land, which had been bulldozed to provide the location for yet another group of buildings for the expanding Shanghai market. The knoll had been constructed by bulldozers, which had heaped earth as the field below was leveled. From it, they had a clear line of sight to the complex and could make out three low watch towers with armed sentries in each.

They searched out a vantage point and were a little surprised to find a small wooden packing crate resting on the ground and covered by some of the local vegetation. They did not pay much attention to it.

Donna observed the building complex through night vision binoculars, "Three watch towers, one over the main gate in and out. If we come in as electrical techs, we'll enter through that gate, and when we free our hacker, we'll need to exit the same way. If we're discovered before we make it out of there, those guards in the towers will cut us to ribbons. They have heavy machine guns and have undoubtedly rehearsed such an action."

They discussed various impediments they would face and were getting nowhere. Then a new voice entered the conversation.

"Perhaps a partnership would be useful."

The Purple Frog team froze for an instant and then dropped to the ground and took up firing positions.

McKnight looked around, but did not see the person who had made the offer. Whoever it was, he spoke English with a British accent. But there was no one visible.

"Show yourself," McKnight called softly.

"Now, why would I do that? Actually, I have all of you covered and can take you out before you'll even know what's happening."

"You're British?"

"Sort of."

McKnight realized they were at a disadvantage. They were caught. However, the situation was confusing. The man who'd spoke had not already opened fire and had offered help with the mission.

McKnight looked around and swept his Glock to cover the area. "Let me guess. You're here with the same goal we have. You want to remove a hacker from the People's Republic."

The British voice responded, "You may be right."

McKnight tried to determine where the voice was coming from but failed. The knoll was clear, and there was no one in sight. The only possible hiding place was in the wooden box they had seen when they arrived, but that was far too small to hide a person. Michael asked, "Are you MI6? CIA?"

"No. I'm a freelancer. I assume you're CIA."

"We aren't CIA, and freelancer sounds like a good descriptor for us as well." Michael was playing for time and Donna was also furtively looking about, trying to identify the location of the unknown party.

The person spoke again. "This is a very tricky operation. Perhaps we could combine forces and help each other out."

McKnight rapidly thought through the scenario. An ad hoc partnership might make sense. The Purple Frog team was certainly short on several needed resources. There was a strong likelihood of a double-cross when they accomplished the mission, but

McKnight was facing too many inhibitors to a successful rescue. An interim combination might have value.

"I'm laying down my weapon, and my team will do the same. Come on out and let's talk." McKnight signaled to his team, and they laid their Glocks on the ground. They all knew that the unknown party probably had them covered, so giving up their weapons did not alter the situation.

The wooden crate moved to one side revealing a hole dug into the earth in which a man stood. He climbed out of the hole carrying an AK47.

"You can call me Abdul. Whom am I addressing?"

Chapter Twenty-Five

McKnight gasped. Was this the assassin he had crossed paths with before? Nothing he'd learned about Abdul would have surprised him. Purple Frog had even used the man for a few missions.

Abdul laid down his rifle and looked over at Michael and his team.

"We both appear to have the same objective, and some deficiencies in our resources to pull it off. Let's see if we can help each other out."

McKnight looked around at the barren and exposed landscape and suggested, "Let's go somewhere a little less obvious and talk."

Abdul nodded. "I agree. I'm staying at the Novotel Shanghai Atlantis. Room eight oh four. Let's meet there. In twenty minutes?"

"Agreed."

As Weber drove them to the hotel, McKnight put a call through to Alan Harlan. It was midday in Virginia, and Alan was in his office when the call came through.

"Morning, Alan."

"Good night, Michael. How's it going?"

"An interesting development."

"Do tell."

"We were checking out the facility and met an old friend."

"Oh? Who?"

"Abdul."

"The assassin?"

"I think so."

"Good God!"

"I wouldn't call him God, and he's certainly not good."

"What's he doing in Shanghai?"

"The same as we are: trying to get the coder out."

"Is he under contract? Why is he doing it?"

"Don't know."

"What does he want?"

"Well, he suggested a partnership. The current resources we have here are not going to cut it. He might have more and better means available, and a joint operation might have a better chance."

"Perhaps. There could be synergy, but you need to make sure that if you are successful and rescue Young that Abdul doesn't take him from you, leaving us back at square one."

"I hear you."

"You're on the ground, Michael, so it's your decision."

"I'll hear him out and then decide."

"Good. Keep me appraised."

McKnight sat opposite the assassin in his hotel room. They had talked for an hour.

McKnight had taken a few notes and he consulted his writing pad. "Let's summarize. Our plan is to knock out their main electric systems and then masquerade as technicians sent in to fix the problem. We'll locate the room the hacker is being held in and free him. We'll escape through the main gate still disguised as electric workers. Simple."

McKnight gave a short laugh and then continued.

"There are a lot of flaws in our plan. We have no one inside to sabotage the main power system. We have no Chinese members of our team to pose as technicians. We don't know where Young is being held, and getting out will probably get us killed, shot from the watch towers. Apart from these little issues, it's a walk in the park."

Abdul gave a matching laugh. "I also have deficiencies. The team I have comprise Chinese thugs, and they're not smart enough to pull off the rescue itself. But, I have someone inside who could trigger the electrical fault and others who can masquerade as the power utility technicians. I also know exactly where this Young guy is being held. And I can take out the guards in the watch towers from my little spot up on the knoll. I have an M82 in my hole; they will never see the shots coming."

McKnight nodded. "What about getting him out of China?"

"The gang I have here is skilled at smuggling. They'll move him through North Korea and then south to another Asian country."

"North Korea? Are you mad? If Kim gets his hands on our hacker's secret, the whole world will be at risk."

"Do you have a better plan?"

"Yes. It's all set up." McKnight told the assassin that he had access to a cargo ship which carried containers, including one that was specially fitted to hide people. His mind went back to having used the

SS Anaconda when he'd rescued Henry Ju-long and his family.

"The container will be loaded with others and the cargo ship will sail out of port and onwards to a country of our choice," McKnight continued.

"Which country?"

"The U.S."

Each man wondered if he could trust the other, but it was clear that without teaming up, the likelihood of success was slim. They would get Young out and then face the next challenge of who would take ownership of the hacker.

"Let me check this out with my boss," McKnight said.

"Fine," Abdul replied. "I'll talk with my partner back home."

Michael McKnight's orders from Silvia Lewis were clear: rescue Mike Young and take him to a CIA safe house in Los Angeles. Lewis and Harlan had finalized the arrangement for the safe house with the CIA director, and she had also agreed that Purple Frog would have one week to quiz the hacker and glean information that might be useful to their organization. During that time, Tina and Silvia would discuss how the hacker's code would be used by the U.S. government.

Tina was probably not sure what that meant and was skeptical. The solution to the president's dilemma rested with the clandestine organization that she knew as Well-wisher, and she knew this was her only hope of preventing the destruction of the CIA's data worldwide, so she had agreed to the terms.

After leaving Abdul's hotel, McKnight made another call to Harlan, who had Lewis join him. He told them about the operational details of the rescue and the Purple Frog management agreed that the combination had a far better chance of a successful rescue than each working alone.

Lewis had used the assassin in the Venezuela conflict, but was amazed that he had turned up in China.

"What does he want to get out of this?" she asked.

"We haven't discussed that yet, but my guess is that it's money. He seems to have an inside source in the Cyber Offensive group and probably heard about the code's ransomware potential."

"You're probably right. Does he know about Yang's threat and the deadline?"

"No, and I don't intend to enlighten him."

"Good call. The less he knows, the better,"

McKnight then raised an important issue. "He's going to ask or demand something, and I'll need to be able to answer him. What shall I tell him about what he can have?"

A half hour later, he called the number Abdul had provided him.

"I've spoken to my boss and our partnership is approved," McKnight said.

"Good. I spoke with my partner, and she likes the idea as well. So, partner, let's meet early tomorrow morning and discuss the details."

The next morning, McKnight and his team met with Abdul and his Chinese gang at a small warehouse owned by the gang. Michael asked Abdul to meet with him alone for a few minutes, and the other members of each team left the main area and collected some cold beers.

McKnight looked Abdul up and down. "You and I nearly met several years back in Brussels. We missed you by a few minutes, as I recall."

"That was a long time ago. Were you people responsible for that fake abort code?"

"Yes."

The two men looked at each other and thought back to that mission.

McKnight saw a man who was a lot younger than he had expected, probably in his early thirties. McKnight was now forty-eight, but fit, and easily up to the challenge that they would face in the next few days.

Abdul raised the issue that Michael had been expecting.

"Let's say we get lucky and break this hacker out. What happens to him then? Do you keep him and have him use his special code so you can make a bunch of money? Do you turn him over to the U.S. government, the CIA? I'm putting my men and myself on the line for this operation, and I need to know what the upside will be for us."

Michael nodded. "What's your interest in the hacker?"

"That's not hard. Money. Cash. Dollars. Lots of dollars."

"How much? One time payout."

Abdul was caught off guard. He had discussed the idea with Betty, but had not discussed an amount which would be acceptable. Before the partnership, they'd thought they would make that decision when they freed the hacker and took control of his ability to extort cash. Maybe they would just keep the gig going year after year until the authorities found a way to inhibit the code's destructive power. Now McKnight was asking for an amount that would satisfy the assassin. Perhaps the African American's organization would pay cash up front rather than allow Abdul to take the hacker. It would certainly be simpler.

"I want to think about that." He knew he would have to discuss the matter further with Betty. She would agree with what he decided, but needed to be involved in the decision.

McKnight looked the assassin in the eyes. "Okay. Here's the deal. You and your team will work with us and together we'll spring Young. We have the way of getting him out of China and into the U.S. Then you'll have a week where he works for you and gets you what you want. It'll only be one shot, so what you make from that, you keep, but after that, we're done. Of course, Young might decide not to work with you, but we can always threaten to return him to the Chinese."

Abdul nodded his acceptance. At the back of his mind was the sum of one hundred million U.S. dollars, and from what he knew of the ransomware approach, the one shot that McKnight had offered could net that amount. He already had a functioning money laundering chain in place, which he'd used for his assassination fees, so that part was taken care of. He wondered what Betty's reaction would be to the one hundred million number.

McKnight continued. "Oh, and one other thing. This caper looks to me like a retirement party for Abdul the assassin. As part of the deal, we want to be able to call on your special skills for a limited set of missions over the next five years."

"But you'll pay me for that separately, right?"

"Yes."

"Then agreed."

Chapter Twenty-Six

That evening, the two groups assembled a half mile outside the Cyber Offensive complex.

Abdul brought McKnight up to date. "I had Yee meet with our inside contact and instruct him on how to fuse the electric system. He will do that at 7:00 p.m. tonight and we'll wait for them to call Shanghai Electric and dispatch their maintenance people. They'll come to the facility by the shortest route from their depot. My people will intercept them and we'll change places. My Chinese team, two of them, will be up front in the van and your team will be in the back. Everyone will wear Shanghai Electric uniforms. Yee has procured uniforms for you. Probably not a great fit, but that shouldn't matter. You'll wear masks—blame COVID. Very common after the recent outbreak. The whole of Shanghai was locked down until a month or two back."

"How many techies would there normally be?" McKnight asked, raising an important issue.

"Probably only two or three, but we'll say that the others are trainees and are along to learn their new trade."

Abdul briefed his Chinese gang, instructing them that McKnight was in charge and they should do whatever he ordered them to do.

Just after 7:00 p.m., the lights at the facility flickered for less than a minute, but then resumed full brightness as the generators kicked in. Half an hour later, a van from Shanghai Electric came down the road in front of the joint team. McKnight had brought the P90 submachine guns for his team. The Chinese gang carried knives and QSZ-92 handguns.

Two of the Chinese men stepped in front of the van and waved for it to stop. Not wishing to run down these men, the driver of the van halted the vehicle and leaned out to ask what the problem was. A half dozen Chinese men emerged from the shadows and pointed their handguns at the technical crew in the van.

Less than five minutes later, they had tied up and gagged the van's occupants and the team entered the vehicle, ready to drive to the Cyber Offensive campus. Abdul remained behind and quickly moved to his sniper hideout on the knoll where he had a clear line of fire on the watch towers.

Two of the Chinese gang members sat up front in the van and McKnight, Strickland, Weber, and

Harness sat in the back with the tools and other equipment. Strickland had dyed her hair from its natural blonde to black, and had constantly complained about having to do this. The whole team wore masks.

At the main gate, the van was expected, and two guards came out of the gatehouse to greet the Shanghai Electric technicians. They also wore masks, and their search of the van was perfunctory. McKnight surmised that Mike Young and his malware code was a secret known only to a few, and the guards, although they had been instructed to strengthen their security protocols, did not see the reason for this and largely ignored it. The power outage was minor, and a quick response from the utility company would be regarded as a routine occurrence.

As expected, the gate guards spoke in Mandarin and looked back toward McKnight's team, no doubt wondering why there were so many technicians. The Chinese driver replied, and McKnight assumed he was explaining that they were trainees. A group of three guards was called to accompany the Shanghai Electric party, and they escorted them to the main electrical building. There they produced a key, unlocked the entrance, and admitted them to the switching room. They stood back and smoked while the two Chinese technicians explained to the trainees, in Mandarin, how such things worked. The trainees—the Purple Frog members of the team—did not understand a word of the language, but kept their heads lowered and nodded enthusiastically.

One of the guards made a comment, motioning to McKnight and the other two male trainees. The Chinese gang member laughed and replied. McKnight expected this was to do with their height, which would be uncommon for Chinese men even in the twenty-first century.

The guard walked over to Weber and was about to question him directly when the technician stepped forward and slid a long knife into his neck, severing his jugular. The guard gargled a little and died. At the same time, the second technician executed a similar action on another guard and Paul Weber took care of the third.

Yee gave some rapid instructions to his gang companion, who had posed as the second technician, and the man turned and set off back towards the gate house.

"Where's he going, Yee?" McKnight asked.

"He go to gate and will take out gate guards when we leave here."

McKnight nodded.

He and his team had memorized the plans of the facility, and using Abdul's diagrams, they knew how to get to the location where they expected to find the hacker.

Dressed as electric company technicians and carrying toolboxes and papers, they passed several guards without being challenged. The P90 submachine guns were folded and lay in the boxes they carried in place of the tools that they had left in the van.

A few conversations in Chinese were handled by the leader of Abdul's group.

They entered the main building and climbed the stairs to the second floor, where the plans showed three rooms comprising a cell, a room for interrogation, and a computer laboratory.

As they opened the door leading from the stairs to the corridor, they saw a guard with a submachine gun slung over his shoulder, looking tired and bored. He stood in front of what they knew to be the interrogation room.

The guard was annoyed. It was near the end of his shift, and in his ten years of service, he had never faced any situation that put him at risk. He shuddered, knowing that inside the room behind him, the sadistic interrogator was, no doubt, torturing the British woman for no purpose.

As he gazed out into the empty corridor, he noticed something odd. The CCTV camera aimed at his location was not showing its normal green light. Probably faulty. He resented this camera, which covered his every action, displaying his movements, whatever they were, to a captain in the master control room. The camera had never failed before, but he did not think too much about it. Instead, he thought of ending his shift, returning home, drinking a glass of whisky, and eating a bowl of Hunan beef. Then he felt the sharpness of a knife speeding up from his throat into his brain.

The Purple Frog team had fused the security cameras on the second floor and emerged from the stairwell. The Chinese gang member had dealt the lethal blow to the guard, and they tried the door behind where the guard had stood. It was locked.

Donna rattled the door handle, but it did not budge, "The guard probably has a key."

They searched him and found what they were looking for in his uniform pocket. After opening the door, they entered. Mike Young was not there, but in a chair, manacled, sat the bloodied body of a half-naked woman. Beside her was a Chinese man with a sergeant's insignia wearing a leather apron.

The man raised his hands as Donna covered him with her submachine gun.

Donna looked about the room. The man's apron was covered with a significant amount of fresh blood, and on a table close by was a set of sharp instruments which Donna surmised were his.

Her thoughts were interrupted.

"No more. Please, no more." The woman's voice was soft and compliant, and evidenced the pain her wounds were giving her.

Donna Strickland had, over the years, seen many pitiful sights when humans had subjected other humans to despicable acts. In fact, Donna had administered many wounds in defense, attack, or in a dozen cases, torture to extort vital information. But the sight of the woman hit her. She had been blinded, and her face and breasts were lacerated. Her fingers, which were secured in manacles, had been smashed.

With a hammer? Donna vomited.

"Who's there?" the woman, unseeing, seemed to sense that the people who had entered the cell were different than her torturers.

"We're here to get you out," Donna said.

The woman turned towards the voice and let out a moan.

"Who are you?"

"It doesn't matter who we are. We'll get you out." Donna looked at the woman again. "Who are you? Are you with Mike Young?"

"Yes. The bloody Chinese thought I was the hacker and they found Mike through me." She struggled to speak through the pain she was suffering. "I gave him up. I'm not proud of what I did, but I was so scared they would hurt me." Her head drooped. "Now look at me. Look what the bastards did to me just to make him do their bidding."

Donna had recovered a little and gazed in silence at the programmer. The sergeant started to edge towards the door, but Donna saw his move and waved him back.

Then she turned back to the woman. "Don't worry. We'll get you out."

The tortured hacker nodded and then seemed to reach a conclusion. "Look at me. They blinded me, and they smashed my fingers so I can't use a keyboard or a computer again. I'm useless and I deserve it. I sold out my friend. I just want to die. End it. Just end it. Kill me, please. *Please.*"

Donna understood.

"Please, please, please. Kill me."

Donna could tell that it was unlikely the woman would survive an attempt to rescue her, and looking at the wounds and the infection in many of them, she judged that the woman had only a day or two of life left regardless. She made up her mind and sent a single bullet into the woman's brain.

She then turned to the sergeant. "Your handiwork?" He nodded slowly and it was obvious he knew he would soon be dead as well.

"Let's not make this too easy," she said, and sent a short burst of bullets into the man's groin. He screamed with pain. "You're going to bleed out. Death should take about twenty minutes, maybe thirty. Think on what you've done, you bastard." The man slumped to the floor, writhing, and continued to scream.

McKnight had entered the cell and watched, without passion, as Donna shot the interrogator.

"Lucky this cell has been soundproofed," he said. "Otherwise, we'd already have half the Chinese army here by now."

Dang Huan was not at the facility. He was at his home eating his evening meal with his wife and two sons. In the background, music played from an American

Alexa device, and he felt content and thrilled at his likely promotion, coupled with the success of the malware he had procured. The U.S. still had two days to agree to the ultimatum for them to not challenge China's increased deployment in the South China Sea. Dang had little to do for the next day or two, so he had left the complex at 6:00 p.m. and returned home.

Since the power outage had been short and the UPS on the computers did not let them lose power for even a second, no one thought to contact the colonel.

A second key they had taken from the guard opened the door next to the interrogation cell. Inside, the room was filled with computing hardware, and McKnight surmised that this was the operations center for the delete code. There was nobody in the room, and although it was locked from the outside, it did not have a guard.

A voice came from a location further down the corridor and around a corner. As could be expected, it spoke in Mandarin.

McKnight queried his Chinese teammate. "What's he saying?"

"He bitching about having guard Englishman when everyone else go home."

"Who's he speaking to?"

"Guard who was here. Guard I killed. I fix."

The Chinese man walked the ten feet to the end of the corridor, turned the corner, and carried out a rapid conversation with the guard. McKnight listened to hear the outcome and then heard a grunt and the sound of a man falling to the floor, along with the clatter of his submachine gun as it hit the concrete.

They searched the second guard and found a key to the third room. Inserting it into the lock, they opened the door. Upon entering, they found the lights on and Mike Young looking haggard, unshaven, and in need of a shower. He cowered in the corner on a narrow bed and showed his expectation of some further harassment.

"Hello. You must be Mike Young," McKnight said.

Mike was disoriented. "Yes. I am."

McKnight used a picture of the hacker that Ching Tong had lifted from the internet to confirm Young's identity.

"We're here to rescue you." The team removed the masks they had been wearing.

"Oh, my God."

"Is it true you developed this delete code?"

The hacker breathed in relief. Then he paused. Could this be a trick by Dang Huan? But the man in front of him and his companions were obviously Caucasian.

He answered cautiously. "Yes."

"Can the Chinese use it without you?"

"No. Only I have access."

"So, without you, the code is worthless?"

"That's right." Young hesitated, realizing that he had just made a case for the armed African American standing in front of him to terminate his life.

"We don't have time to talk now, so let's get you out of here. We'll fill you in later. Do everything I tell you to. Nothing else. Understand?"

"Yes." Mike sighed with relief that they were talking rescue and not killing him.

"Let's go."

"Wait. I need my laptop. I have everything about the code on that. It's in the computer room."

They went to the operations room and Mike snatched up his laptop, disconnecting the links to the other computers in the room. He pocketed the power cord and tucked the computer under his arm.

McKnight asked, "Got everything?"

"Yes. Everything we need."

Chapter Twenty-Seven

In a control room on the lower floor of the main building, a man in uniform with an insignia identifying his rank of captain was monitoring the security cameras and realized that those on the second floor were not operating. *Probably due to that outage,* he thought. However, he decided to check in with the guards on duty on that floor. He knew there was a special and secret operation being played out in the complex and the second floor was where it was headquartered.

Calling the radios of each guard, he received no reply, so he sent a team of five armed men to check out the situation. They reported back that the guards were missing, but each of the rooms was still locked. The captain sent up a set of master keys and alerted Dang Huan at his home, who let out a curse and called for his car before terminating the call.

Meanwhile, the captain in the control room raised the alarm as his first response team entered the interrogation room and found the British woman dead, along with the two guards. They also found Dang Huan's interrogator, who was alive but still in agony.

The guard leading the team had little regard for the sergeant, whom he knew to be a sadistic brute. He looked at the woman's mutilated body and then at the dying sergeant. He spat on the man. "Serves you right." Then he reported back to his captain.

The captain called Dang Huan again and updated him on the situation.

"Captain, where is the foreign prisoner?" Dang Huan asked.

The captain did not know of the prisoner and replied, "We did not find anyone else."

"Damn it! He is very important. Find him, but keep him safe. He's no good to me dead."

The captain ordered the search area to be widened and dispatched several more teams. In a dumpster in the car park, one of his teams found the three dead guards who had accompanied the technicians from the electric company. The captain now spearheading the search for the intruders and the missing foreigner raised the alarm status to the highest level, which included a total lockdown of the facility.

He spoke calmly into his radio. "It's the Shanghai Electric team. They are trying to abduct a foreigner who is very important to us. Capture them, but do not harm the foreigner."

McKnight and his team, along with the British hacker and the Chinese gang, ran down the steps to ground level and were about to leave the building when a squad of six guards carrying QCQ-171 submachine guns came around the corner facing them. McKnight sent a hail of bullets towards them and two were hit. The others took what cover there was and returned fire. McKnight wished he had a grenade, but since he did not, he hoped the attacking force did not, either.

The Chinese guards fired several volleys and McKnight wondered if they carried spare magazines. If they did not, they would not be able to sustain the fight much longer before running short of ammunition. He recognized the weapons they were using, and knew each held a magazine of thirty rounds. While submachine guns were normally not on issue to the military, who did not see value in such a short-range weapon, it and the QSZ-92 handgun were the police weapons of choice, and the guards had obviously adopted them.

The Chinese thugs with McKnight also showed little sense in expending ammunition and soon they ran out. McKnight, Strickland, Weber, and Harness had a more sensible and disciplined tactic and waited until the firing subsided.

A man with the rank of corporal appeared and took charge of the guards. He shouted at his men in Mandarin.

McKnight spoke to Yee. "What's he saying?"

"He has told them to stop firing. He is worried they might hit the prisoner."

The guards assumed they had superior firepower and moved forward to capture McKnight's group, but when they were halfway along the corridor where there was no cover, the Purple Frog team fired short bursts into their foe. All five men died instantly, but one of the two who had been wounded in the initial skirmish returned fire and caught Donna in the side with a single bullet. Weber killed the man, and when the other wounded guard raised his weapon, Harness killed him as well.

The Purple Frog team were wearing lightweight Kevlar vests under their Shanghai Electric uniforms, but the 9mm parabellum round had punctured the seam of her vest and entered Donna's side. The bullet was still inside her.

"Oh, fuck. That hurts." Donna dropped to the floor and McKnight motioned Weber to pick her up as they left the building and made for the van.

When they reached the vehicle, Weber removed a field surgical dressing and applied it to Donna's wound. "That'll stop the bleeding, but we need to get the bullet out."

She turned to her boss. "Michael, promise me you won't let me die with black hair while wearing this crappy uniform."

"I promise."

On reaching the van, McKnight found two guards. He was surprised that they were standing about rather than taking up defensive positions, but he reasoned the communications about the break-in must not have conveyed the threat from the intruders. A few short bursts from his Belgium submachine gun killed them before they had a chance to even raise their weapons.

Weber laid Donna on the floor in the back of the van and McKnight took the driver's seat with Tom Harness next to him. The others entered through the back door and sat on the benches lining it.

"I'd say we have five minutes to get out of here." McKnight started the engine, and in the back, Mike Young, still in shock from his recent rescue and the killing he had just observed, looked about and realized that his friend was not with them. "What about Cate? She was with me here. Did you find her?"

Weber reached over and placed a hand on his arm. "Cate? Was that her name? I'm sorry. She didn't make it."

They drove slowly toward the main gate just as sirens shattered the still night and a group of experienced guards rushed to follow their trained response to the emergency. From the driver's seat of the van, McKnight could see that they were well disciplined. While in many cases guards would assume the situation was just a drill to keep them on their toes and would not take the threat seriously, these elite guards in the Cyber Offensive facility did anything but.

The Chinese gang member who'd left McKnight's team before they'd entered the main building had walked quietly to the guardhouse at the main gate. Before the alarm had been raised, he'd entered and carried out an animated conversation with the two occupants about the rising prices of food in the Chinese city. When the alarm was sounded, each guard had turned his gaze to the control screens in front of them and the gang member had withdrawn a pistol and shot each of them in the head. On one security camera screen, he saw the Shanghai Electric van driving slowly toward the gate, and he activated a button which started to open it.

Above him, he knew the guards in the watch towers were aware that the van was to be stopped. They would be training their heavy caliber machine guns on the area just outside the gate as the van passed through.

Dang Huan was in his car and speeding towards the facility. He shouted into his phone at the captain who had just provided him an update. "Do not kill anyone. The foreign hacker is fundamental to China and must be protected at all costs. I repeat, do not shoot at these people. Shoot the tires of the van and its engine, but do not—I repeat, do not—harm any passengers."

The main gate was now open, and McKnight slowed the van to allow the gang member who had opened their escape route to climb onboard. He then accelerated out into the night. McKnight called Abdul on his cell phone to give him an update. He knew that above the gate, each of the three machine gunners would be setting their sights on the van, and he waited for bullets to fly into the vehicle.

Half a mile away, Abdul had hoped that McKnight's team would be able to complete their mission without raising an alarm. Hearing the commotion and having McKnight confirm that they were being pursued and would exit through the main gate imminently, he took up his position and killed each of the tower guards with large caliber bullets from his M82 sniper rifle.

"Piece of cake." Abdul packed up his weapon and walked quickly to a waiting SUV, which took him away from the scene to meet with the others in an empty building.

When he arrived, Abdul noticed that Donna was hurt.

"Was she hit?"

"Yes," McKnight said. "We need a doctor. Can your people organize one?"

"I'll try." Abdul called over to Yee and passed on the request.

The man nodded. "No problem, but take time. I call now. Maybe tomorrow."

"That's too late. It must be in the next hour."

"Okay, okay."

He accessed his cell phone and made a call. As he was waiting for the call to be picked up, he turned to Abdul. "Cost more money. Okay?"

Abdul replied, "Yes."

They abandoned the Shanghai Electric van and switched the team to Abdul's SUV and another Wuling Hongguang vehicle. They left the site before a city-wide alert could be issued and roadblocks initiated. Driving to the Port of Shanghai docks, they located the correct container in the yard and met the Chilean, Captain Flores.

"Welcome again." He addressed McKnight, whom he had met several years previously when he had smuggled Henry Ju-long and his family out of China. "Your usual accommodation?" The captain motioned to the open door of the shipping container.

An hour later, a short Chinese man with multiple facial scars arrived at the port on a motor bike. He was met by one of the gang members and escorted to the container.

In the back of the steel box, there was a roll-out bed, and Donna lay on it. McKnight had already administered some painkillers, which had sent her into a drowsy mode.

"It still hurts like hell, but it's quite a buzz," she said.

The doctor took up his bag and removed a number of items. He did not speak English, but Yee translated between him, McKnight, and Donna.

McKnight was concerned. "Is he a real doctor, Yee?"

"Yes. Very important surgeon."

"But he works for your gang?"

"He like gamble and owe us lot of money. He provides service when we want."

The doctor had spent a few minutes inspecting the wound and was shaking his head.

"Is it serious? Ask him," McKnight said.

Yee did so.

"Is serious. Should have hospital, but I tell him not possible."

The doctor administered some drugs, and as Donna sank into sleep, he started to probe for the bullet. Five minutes later, the slug, still covered in Strickland's blood, rested on a plate next to her reclined body. The doctor wiped his hands and started to sew up the wound.

"Not very hygienic," McKnight said.

Yee conveyed this to the doctor, who grunted and motioned to the inside of the container before voicing a string of curses in Chinese.

Yee translated, "He says compared with filthy container, he very clean."

The doctor handed over some dressings, antibiotics, and painkillers.

McKnight bowed to the man and thanked him. He nodded back.

After the doctor had loaded up his medical bag and departed, Yee and his men took their leave. Abdul thanked them and told them they would be well paid for their work and the risks they'd taken.

Captain Flores, who had witnessed the operation, shrugged and told McKnight that it was time to close up, and that when the container was next opened, they would be on the high seas.

The sealed container was transported to the dock and loaded to the SS Anaconda with several others.

Twelve hours later, they reached international waters and Captain Flores opened the container, allowing the occupants to leave and enter the main salon of the ship. They did not want to move Donna, so they left her in the bed in the container, but with the doors open to allow light and fresh air to enter the space.

Abdul used the captain's satellite phone to call a number in Nigeria, which connected through a few other countries to Betty in KL.

"Brad. You okay?" she asked after picking up.

"Yes, darling. I am fine."

"Success?"

"Yes."

"You have hacker. Yes?"

"Yes. I want to discuss the deal I made on our behalf."

On day two, Donna reacted to her wound with a high temperature and fever.

"I'm going to fucking die out here, aren't I?"

McKnight tried to comfort her, but she continued, "My hair is black. I can't die. I want my blonde back."

"Donna, stop whining. Rest and take these meds. You'll be fine."

She took the tablets and sank into a troubled but deep sleep.

Michael feared for her well-being, but within a day—with the help of the antibiotics—the fever broke, and a day later she was feeling better and delivering the repartee that was her trademark.

"When can I wash my bloody hair?"

The voyage took a week, and McKnight used the time to converse with Abdul, his strange ally. Before they were at sea, everything had happened quickly with little time for any of the team members to get to know Abdul and his motivations. McKnight thought he could trust him, but wasn't sure. As they'd waited, sealed in the container, the quarters had been cramped, and for the hours before they were at sea and the container doors opened, most of them had sat in silence, inhaling the minimal air which came from small vents in the side of the container.

After they were in international waters and the captain deemed it safe, they had emerged, and McKnight decide to take the opportunity to quiz the assassin.

He motioned for the man to join him and walked to an area on the deck where they could sit and converse.

The two men stared at each other. Both were killers, but each came with different motivations and values.

"Tell me about yourself, Abdul," McKnight said.

"Now, why would I do that?"

"It's going to be a long trip to the U.S., and it'll be pretty boring if you don't communicate with us." McKnight had brought a couple of beers with him from the refrigerator in the galley, and he offered one to Abdul. The assassin accepted it, removed the cap, and took a slurp.

"I'm intrigued," McKnight continued. "Your name is Abdul, but you have a British accent. London, I'd say. What am I missing here?"

"I am Afghan. My mother was from Kabul, but she told me my father was American. I never met him, and for all I know, he's dead."

"But the British accent?"

"I needed to blend in. My jobs were in Europe, so I adopted a British accent as a cover. I used a speech coach."

Abdul finished his beer.

"I think you know what I do," he continued, "and your outfit has used me for a couple of projects. But I don't know much about you. Are you CIA?"

"No. We're private, but we parallel the CIA. We operate with a lot fewer restrictions."

"Do you kill people?"

"When necessary."

"You're just like me."

McKnight looked at the assassin.

"No, Abdul. We're not just like you. We only kill when we have to, and then we only target..." He paused trying to think of the right phrase. "Bad guys."

"How do you decide if someone is a bad guy?"

"It's usually easy."

"So, someone directs you. Mister X is a bad guy. Kill him."

McKnight was starting to become annoyed by this assassin, whom he had already classified as a "bad guy."

"That's usually the case. We also have an advisory board that authorizes the action. It's not perfect, but has worked well in practice."

"I'm the same. Someone wants someone else killed and they pay me to do it."

"But you don't care who your target is or why they should be terminated."

"Correct. I don't want to overthink these things."

"Doesn't it bother you?"

"No. I grew up in a war—Afghanistan—and did what I was told. I was a sniper then and I still am. I learned to take the emotion out of killing. It's just a job."

McKnight shook his head. Killing did not bother him either, but he used a moral compass for his actions. He decided that he and Abdul could never be friends, but the assassin did have useful skills.

Over the next few days, their conversation avoided contentious areas and was about the mechanics of various actions each had undertaken rather than focusing on the targets. Each was careful not to share too much with the other. They spent a lot of time on neutral subjects, such as the pros and cons of various weapons. Abdul did not reveal where he lived, nor mention Betty Lau, and Michael did not tell the assassin more about Purple Frog.

Chapter Twenty-Eight

The CIA director was in the middle of a meeting about the delete code and was addressing what options the CIA had if the president decided to reject Yang's demands. When a call came in on her personal phone and she saw the caller ID, she terminated the meeting and sent everyone back to their desks. As she closed her office door, she let out a breath and prayed that this would be good news. She picked up the call.

"Tina," the voice said, "I have good news."

Tina sat down and held the phone firmly to her ear.

Well-wisher continued, "My team has rescued Mike Young from the Chinese."

"God. That's terrific. Where is he?"

"He's currently on the open seas in international waters. The president can tell Yang to go to hell."

"Are you sure about this? What about the code? Does China still have that?"

"Good news on that as well. The hacker tells us that the Chinese cannot activate the code, since he recovered his laptop with the triggering dashboard. They have no way of doing anything without that."

"Wow. That's fantastic."

Then a cloud descended on Tina Graham. "If he's in international waters, can't the Chinese recapture him? If they can, anything we do may be premature."

"We don't think there is any risk of that. You told me Yang set a deadline for the U.S. response, and Young will still be at sea when that time limit expires. You'll have to take my word that he is out of Chinese control."

"I don't like it. I don't want to tell the president that we have eradicated the threat if Yang could still follow through on it."

"All I can say is that we believe the threat has been eliminated. Tell the president what I have told you. If you don't tell him, he'll be making a choice without this knowledge. He might give in to Yang without needing to."

Tina thought about her options and decided to take Well-wisher's advice and tell the president what she knew. He would obviously ask her where she had received the information and who had staged the rescue. He would also demand that Young became a "guest" of the United States government, where he would hand over access to the code. If she told him about Well-wisher, he would ask her how much she trusted this external, clandestine group, and she would confirm that they were to be believed. What she did not want, but was likely, was that he would want to know a lot more about the clandestine group.

She called her personal assistant and asked him to set up a meeting with the president. Explaining the relationship and admitting that she did not even know what the group was called would not be well received, but the news would be.

The private jet landed at St. Croix's airport and Jason Overly walked out to it as it taxied to a halt. The door of the plane opened and two attractive women in their late twenties and an older woman in her fifties exited, stepping down from the aircraft.

"Hi, Dad," the two younger women said in unison, and Jason rushed forward, embracing each of them.

"How's Mom?" Olivia asked.

"It's close. Doctor Stephens says it will probably be in the next week."

The older woman, Sarah's sister Elsie, had a grim expression on her face and said, "Hello, Jason."

"Hello, Elsie." He embraced his sister-in-law.

Darnell, Jason's bodyguard and driver, took the women's cases and loaded them into the SUV. They entered the vehicle and Darnell drove them to Sugar Ridge on the north shore of the island.

The girls and their aunt spent the next hour with Sarah before she showed exhaustion and drifted off into an unsettled sleep.

"Oh, Dad, she looks awful." Olivia said.

Elsie chimed in, "She's so thin."

This was the fourth trip the younger women had made to visit Sarah, and Elsie had come down to St. Croix on only one other occasion. With each visit, the young women saw a noticeable deterioration in their mother. What had been a vibrant, attractive woman in her early fifties had, in the past several months, become a skeleton with successive weight loss caused by the cancer and her diminished interest in food. Most of her time was spent sleeping, helped by the painkilling drugs that were administered to her.

"Isn't there anything we can do?" August asked.

"No," Jason said. "As we discussed before, we've tried everything. Even the Swiss clinic turned out to be a waste of time. I'm afraid we must accept the inevitable now and keep her as comfortable as we can. She'll be happier having you here again."

"We, or at least one of us, could have been down here the whole time."

"There's nothing you could have done. Doris has been an angel, and Doctor Stephens has kept her pretty much free from pain."

Doris arrived and had been obviously crying. "Good afternoon, my lovelies. Afternoon, Elsie. I've made you cocktails. I dare say you need them. And one for you, Jason," she added.

Jason knew Sarah and Elsie had not been close, and felt that the older sister resented Sarah's fortune in finding and marrying someone who'd become a billionaire. Her own marriage had been tumultuous and had ended three years after it started in a difficult divorce, and she had resisted entanglement with another man for the past thirty years. She was a bitter woman.

They sat in the bar and reminisced about various times in their lives, and in particular, the role Sarah had played in bringing up the girls. Elsie said little, but was obviously feeling helpless.

Jason's elder daughter, Olivia, took the lead. "Dad, do you remember how bitchy I was when I was nine?"

Elsie sneered.

Jason nodded his agreement. "How could I not remember that? You were a real pain in the ass."

"But that was just my age and the hormones and stuff."

The younger daughter, August, said, "I was never bitchy. Was I, Dad?"

Jason realized they were trying to take him out of the funk he was in. As well as dealing with Sarah's illness, he had been missing the family and friends he had in California.

Olivia continued, "One day, Mom took me out of earshot of the two of you and told me to stop being a princess and start behaving myself. Then she told me about sex. I was shocked at what it entailed, and the fact that Mom was telling me."

"You were both quite forward girls," Jason said. "We probably spoiled you—private schools, the best colleges, new cars at sixteen, vacations in Europe, and your own rooms with ensuite bathrooms. That's not to mention the clothes and shoes."

August countered his comments. "But we never had *haute couture*. Mom took us shopping at Marshalls, and we got our shoes from DSW."

Olivia, who was a self-confessed foodie, said, "We used to eat out a lot. And not fast food. It was nearly always some fancy restaurant."

"What about Sunday lunch? We always had that at home, family style," August said.

Jason warmed to the conversation. "You were both really difficult at first. Mom banned cell phones at the table and had these rituals of talking about the events of the week. She also insisted on proper etiquette, manners, and eating food properly. Not just shoveling it down and getting back to games and TV."

August smiled. "At the time, we hated it, but looking back, we had real family time and talked a lot. It was also when we heard all the dad jokes."

Jason had gone along with the banter enough and finally broke down weeping. His daughters hugged him and joined him in crying. Elsie also started to sob.

Later, Jason took Elsie aside. "I know you and Sarah haven't been close over the years, but I'm sure she loves you."

"I don't know why she should. I am the elder sister, but she has always outshone me. She was better at school, she was more athletic, she was more beautiful, and she got into Princeton."

Elsie looked at the pool and the blue of the Caribbean beyond it.

"She married you and was happy," she continued. "I married a jerk and was unhappy until I divorced him. Since then, I've been a miserable, frustrated woman. I don't have friends, and I spend my days resenting my little sister. Now that she's dying, I realize what a fool I've been."

Jason took her in his arms and hugged her.

"Sarah is well aware of the way you felt," he said, "but I think you should go to her now and make up. Tell her what you've just told me. Tell her you've been a fool. Tell her that you love her, and always have."

Elsie nodded and left the pool deck to enter the bedroom, where Sarah was just waking.

Jason did not hear the conversation, but was aware of a lot of tears from both women. He smiled a grim smile.

Elsie emerged from the bedroom and muttered a thanks to Jason for his advice. Crying openly, she went to her room.

Jason visited Sarah and she weakly said, "Elsie? Your doing? Thank you so much for caring." She drifted back into sleep.

Chapter Twenty-Nine

After the escape of the British hacker, Dang Huan faced a problem. He had taken a risk in revealing Young's potential to his president, and Yang had decided to use the delete code in a daring threat to the president of the United States. With the hacker gone and his laptop with him, Dang knew that Yang's bluff would be called and he would be severely embarrassed in his dealings with the American president.

Dang knew he would suffer for his incompetence in allowing the escape. He would undoubtedly face a death sentence, and his demise was unlikely to be a quick and painless one. His mind travelled back to the interrogation room where his sergeant had tortured the British woman, Cate Glover. Initially he'd looked away as the interrogator had sliced into her flesh, but after a while, he'd become fascinated at the pain the man could inflict with such small instruments, and he'd watched the action, feeling an almost sexual thrill from the abuse.

His mind jerked back from the fantasy as his thoughts focused on his own dilemma. The breakout had been reported by the guards in the Cyber Offensive facility and a city-wide search had been conducted, but as Shanghai had a population of twenty-six million, the likelihood of finding the hacker was remote. There was no way to determine who had affected the escape, but the CCTV security footage indicated a mix of Asians and Caucasians in the invading force.

His phone rang, and as he answered it, he felt a foreboding. It was his commanding officer, and the man wanted an explanation. Dang did not have a satisfactory one, and a few minutes later he heard a squad of guards arriving at his office to arrest him. The door was locked from the inside.

"Dang Huan. Open the door," a voice called from the outside.

Dang reached into a drawer in his desk and withdrew his QSZ-92. He checked the magazine and then chambered a round. As the guards broke his door down, he aimed it at his head and pulled the trigger. His last thoughts were not of his wife and children, but of the delete code and its amazing potential.

A few days later, twenty Chinese merchant ferries that had been reconfigured as troop-carrying ships and two Type 055 destroyers, neared Thitu, an island in the South China Sea, which was controlled by the Philippines but claimed by China. The ships were in formation offshore and were preparing to land and offload several thousand military personnel and significant weaponry.

A Chinese admiral was in charge of the overall force, and traveled on the lead destroyer. He scanned the port with binoculars and saw a small contingent of soldiers, who would shortly put up a fruitless attempt to fight off their invaders. He laughed softly and called down to the ship's gunnery officer. "Fire five shells at the back of the dock. Do not damage where the transports will berth."

"Sights set, sir. Will fire on your command."

A sailor scanning the radar motioned his findings to another officer on the bridge of the destroyer, who interrupted the admiral before he could issue the order to fire.

"Sir, we have a lot of indicators on the radar. Looks like a flotilla of ships."

The admiral looked at the radar screen and then turned his binoculars to a spot behind his ship. He saw a string of dots on the horizon.

"Sir," the radar operator called, "the profile is for an aircraft carrier, a cruiser, and a number of destroyers."

The captain was surprised. He had been informed that there would be no other ships in the area and that his attack on the small island would only face a light, local defense. He was about to hail these ships when a message came in.

"Attention Chinese fleet. This is the USS Ronald Reagan. We are accompanied by the USS Theodore Roosevelt, a guided-missile cruiser, two guided-missile destroyers, and a number of other assets. You have entered waters which do not belong to the People's Republic of China. They are owned by other sovereign states, and we have been asked to see that you turn around and return to Chinese waters. Do you comply?"

The admiral immediately communicated with Beijing, and after a few minutes of garbled messages back and forth, he was told that the president's plans had changed. The admiral should lead the fleet back to its base on Hainan Island. He ordered the new directive to be radioed to all the ships in his flotilla and they turned and steamed to the north the way they had come.

In Beijing, the Chinese president was furious. That North Korean weasel, Dang Huan, had lost the British hacker and the delete code. Yang viewed it as the ultimate weapon, and he had no doubt that the code and the hacker were now, somehow, in the hands of the Americans. Communications with his fleet in the South China Sea confirmed that the United States no longer feared the delete code. A call had been received from the American secretary of state, not even the president, that told him in no uncertain terms that the United States no longer regarded the code as a threat.

As well as losing face with the U.S. president, he had burned bridges with his Russian ally.

He was also angry that Dang had committed suicide; he'd had another death in mind.

Yang walked around his office and smashed a number of ornamental pots and statues, many of which had been gifts from the delegates of fawning countries. Then he noticed a bronze statue of a cowboy on a bucking bronco, a gift from the American president on a state visit a year previously. He grabbed it, and realizing that he could not break it easily, he flung it at his large picture window in the Zhongnanhai overlooking the Forbidden City. He had forgotten that the window was made of bullet-proof glass. The statue bounced against the glass and spun back into the room, narrowly missing him. The impact on the window set off alarms and a squad of guards, rifles at the ready, rushed into his office. He looked at them and then sank to the floor, exhausted and frustrated.

For perhaps the first time in weeks, Sarah was both wide awake and in little pain. She knew this was a freak circumstance and temporary, but she smiled across her bed at Jason, who sat on a chair close by. He smiled back.

She spoke in her normal, confident voice. "You have shared all your secrets with me over the years, my love." Then she paused. "Except one."

Jason was taken aback. "I don't understand."

"I'll bet you do." She coughed a little, then continued. "When we were down here during that Venezuelan fiasco, you had McKnight, a man who works for you, rescue me from Sanchez and then capture him. I'm not a fool, Jason. Software companies don't have people with his skills on hand. He certainly wasn't a bodyguard."

Jason turned away and looked out across the pool deck to the sea, remembering the situation.

She continued, "At the time, I wanted to ask you what the truth was, but I trusted that you had a very good reason for keeping it from me. Now, before I go, I'd like to know."

Jason knew he could not deny her the information, but a moment of fear passed through him. *What if she despises me for sponsoring a rogue organization?*

He said in a soft, serious voice, "Eight years ago, I set up an organization separate from Avanch. I call it Purple Frog."

"Purple Frog? What's a purple frog?"

"It's actually a very rare amphibian. It hides in the earth and emerges only once a year to mate. I wanted to have an operation which flew under the radar and only emerged when needed."

"Why did you do that?"

"In many ways, you prompted it. Do you remember the discussions we had, way back, when we talked about the problems of promoting peace in this troubled world?"

"Yes. I remember. We concluded that privacy regulations, political correctness, truth, kindness, tolerance, and the like were major inhibitors in getting things done. The safeguards we had in place to foster our democracy allowed our enemies an advantage."

"Purple Frog bends the rules to foster world peace."

She dropped her head to one side. "Bends the rules or breaks them?"

"Both. We're not perfect, but we try hard to act inside the law when possible. Sometimes that isn't possible. On occasions, we have broken laws to achieve our goal."

"So, you saved the day with the Venezuelans. What else?"

"Quite a lot of things that have been kept very quiet. Two that were public in the end were the Brotherhood of the Skull affair with Gideon Page, and the drone attack on the Nimitz. My people have been very active over the years."

"Did your people assassinate Page?"

He hesitated, but knew he would have to tell her the truth whether she liked it or not.

"Yes. Indirectly but yes."

"Good job." Sarah smiled again, "Kiss me, please."

He did so and the drugs took over. She fell into a peaceful sleep.

Chapter Thirty

When the SS Anaconda docked at the Coronado Navy Base in San Diego, California, three armored SUVs met the vessel and a squad of CIA officers escorted Mike Young, the Purple Frog team, and Abdul to a CIA secure site in the Malibu area.

The house was on a cliff overlooking the Pacific and comprised eight bedrooms, extensive living areas, and a monster kitchen.

"Wow. Our tax dollars at work." Weber shook his head at the expensive dwelling.

McKnight whistled while looking about. "Probably seized from a drug lord."

However, typical of government operations, the interior fell far short of the exterior. What had probably been lavishly furnished by the previous owner had been replaced by less expensive second-hand couches and Ikea cabinetry. The appliances were top of the line, but the kitchen cabinets were in urgent need of replacement.

McKnight nodded to Weber. "Our government often spends our taxes in strange ways."

The house had a bank of security cameras and a monitoring room, and the internet service exceeded typical home systems.

Ching Tong had flown out and was waiting for them when they entered. He offered his hand to the British hacker.

"Hi. You must be Mike." After his recent experience in China, Mike's reaction was to be expected.

"You're Chinese. Michael, what's this about?"

"He's with us, Mike. Just happens to be Chinese."

Mike was skeptical, but after a few minutes chatting with the Purple Frog hacker, he relaxed. He and Ching Tong worked to set up Mike's laptop with the large screen monitors and other computers that the CIA had provided at his request. Ching Tong did not share his real name with Mike.

When the computer was up and running, Mike's first act was to satisfy the agreement that McKnight had made with Abdul. Ching Tong watched him as he ran a ransomware attack on the Swiss Banking Corporation in Basel. He demanded the equivalent of one hundred million dollars in exchange for not destroying the investment accounts and deposits of some of the world's richest and most influential people. He demonstrated the power of his system and the bank acquiesced to his demand. The money was paid through Abdul's network, and he was able to share his success with Betty Lau.

"Brad," Betty said when Abdul called her, "You rich man now. You still want Betty?"

"Absolutely. I thought we might want to buy a yacht and sail through the Malaysian islands. I'm sure we can pick up one of the Russian oligarch's vessels for a rock bottom price. There are a lot of them impounded across the world."

"Bad idea. Too many pirates in these waters. But perhaps I get crew from China who can defend. Maybe we become pirates."

"I want to celebrate with you. I'll be back within a week."

"I want you in my bed, Brad. That where we celebrate."

Over the first few days, Young warmed to Ching Tong. Their mutual interest in programming and hacking was a common ground for them, and each respected the other's skills. Ching Tong managed to keep his ego restrained and he and Mike talked for hours about all aspects of the hacker's skills. Each had stories to tell, but Mike, while brilliant at his craft, had little experience in the real world of hacking. The conversation moved to the delete code and Mike's pride in the system overpowered his natural suspicions about imparting the knowledge to another.

He found his time with Ching Tong a delight after his experience in China, and he had relaxed, telling his fellow hacker about the intricacies of his code. Dang Huan had never praised his skills, just pushed for him to use the code as a weapon, and had taken delight in his cruelty. Mike's mind travelled back to what the colonel had done to Cate, and although he had never really liked her, their cruelty had disgusted him. He knew he was largely to blame; if he had not developed the code, she would have never been kidnapped and tortured. He did not know what had happened after the strange team had brought about his escape from the Chinese, but they had told him that she'd died.

Ching Tong said he found it hard to believe that the piggybacked code had made it through the various checks the software companies used.

"You must've had a lot of luck on your side, Mike."

"I agree. One thing that may have helped was that the senior programmer responsible for the checks at Realizmm was out on maternity leave at the time. There was a zero-day error in the code that the browser companies had to fix in a hurry, so I guess it just crept in through the cracks."

Ching Tong was a little older than the British hacker and dressed well. Mike knew that although the team had found him some new clothes, had his hair trimmed, and he now showered twice a day, to Ching, he probably still had the appearance of a homeless person.

Silvia was in a dilemma. Although she was loyal to the United States, her homeland, she was worried that turning the hacker and his delete code over to the CIA would provide the U.S. administration and military with a weapon they might use wrongly. She was due a call with Tina to discuss how they would proceed, and she wanted to involve Jason in the options she was considering.

She was hesitant to bother Jason as Sarah did not have long to live, and Jason would not want to be pulled away from her at this time. Finally, she concluded that Jason would want to be involved, regardless, so she put through a call to him in St. Croix.

"Jason," she said when he answered. "I feel terrible interrupting your final time with Sarah, but what we do next could determine the world's future. We've faced some real threats before, but this code, in the wrong hands, could change history. In China's hands, the world would have faced domination, but if we hand it and Mike Young over to the U.S. Government, they might also use it inappropriately. I have a talk scheduled with Tina Graham tomorrow, but I still don't know what to say. What to demand."

Jason did not hesitate. "Maybe we should keep the code and the hacker in Purple Frog."

Donna had been flown back to the East Coast and was being treated by one of Purple Frog's medical staff, who visited her in her apartment each day. McKnight, Weber, and Harness were still on the West Coast with Young, safeguarding the hacker as he worked with Ching Tong and explained the code and his magic dashboard. Abdul had departed already.

Weber was keeping watch on the monitors, which showed the exterior of the safehouse, when he saw three vehicles pull into the parking space outside the main entrance. They were marked FBI and a dozen members of a SWAT team left the vehicles and moved towards the house. They all carried assault weapons, which were held ready to shoot, if needed.

"What the..."

Chapter Thirty-One

Weber raised the alarm and McKnight and Harness took up their P90s.

McKnight scanned the security monitors and found one was not working.

Outside, one member of the squad, identifiable as their leader, called out through a bullhorn. "This is the FBI. We have no desire to hurt you or arrest you. If you try to prevent us from doing what we are here to do, we shall retaliate. Be sensible, lay down your weapons, and come out with your hands in the air."

McKnight opened a window and shouted out, "What do you want? We are here as guests of the CIA and have been assured of our safety. You can call Tina Graham, the director."

"She's CIA. We're the FBI and under direct orders from the president. We are taking Michael Young into custody. He's a threat to the United States and we are going to protect our country. Now, I'll repeat, lay down your weapons."

"I'll need to check with my boss."

"No time for that. Don't make me send my men in to get you. Do it easy and no one gets hurt. Do it hard and we'll win." As an afterthought he added, "And you'll die."

Michael started to prepare for a gunfight when he heard a noise behind him. He turned and faced a second squad of FBI officers with assault weapons, all aimed at him, Weber, Harness, Ching Tong, and Mike. He reasoned they had come along the beach and climbed the cliff on the ocean side of the house. McKnight realized the security camera covering this approach had been disabled.

"Paul, Tom, put down your guns." McKnight laid down his as well.

He then directed his attention to the FBI leader, who had entered through the front door.

"Who are you?" McKnight asked. "I want to see your credentials and your arrest warrant."

The leader showed his shield and McKnight took a mental note of his name and the last four digits of his badge number.

"Warrant?"

"We don't need a warrant. We have orders directly from the president."

McKnight was furious, but with the guns trained on him and his men, he had little choice of action.

The FBI held the Purple Frog team at gunpoint and then escorted Young to an armored vehicle at the front of the house. One of them packaged up all the hardware, including Mike's laptop, and carried it to a second vehicle.

The lead agent then addressed McKnight. "We were instructed to thank you for your service to the country and not to harm you. Nor arrest you."

The agents reentered their vehicles and drove away.

"Fuck!" said Michael, reaching for his phone to report to Silvia.

"They didn't harm you or your team?" Silvia asked over the phone.

"No. And they treated Mike Young with kid gloves."

"But they took him, right?"

"Right."

"Are you sure they were FBI and not someone else?"

"I'm not sure, but they seemed real."

Silvia was furious and called Tina immediately after completing her call with McKnight.

"Tina, what the fuck is going on?"

"I've been blindsided. I had to brief the president and he was worried about having Young in the hands of anyone other than the U.S. authorities. I argued with him, but behind my back, he had the attorney general order the FBI to go to the safehouse and take Young. Your people were not to be harmed and were not to be arrested. Young is being brought here to Langley, so he'll be in our custody. Any thoughts you had otherwise are negated."

"You bitch. This is your doing, not the FBI."

"No. It's not mine. I would have probably done the same, but in this case, I was preempted."

Silvia hung up and uttered a scream of rage, which her staff across Purple Frog heard even through the glass walls of her office.

McKnight, Weber, Harness, and Ching Tong returned to Virginia from the Californian safe house as Mike was being flown on a similar route to Langley, where he would be questioned by the spy agency. They both flew in private jets, one funded by the FBI from taxpayer dollars, and one funded by Jason Overly. They took off from the Los Angeles airport a few hours apart and landed at Dulles Airport in Washington. Whereas the Purple Frog team knew where the British hacker was being taken, Mike's FBI escorts had no clue about the other team's destination.

The Purple Frog team took an Uber to a restaurant five miles from the Purple Frog office and was collected there by the organization's driver.

When they arrived, Silvia and Harlan debriefed McKnight first.

"How is Donna?"

"I called the doc on the way back and he says she's doing fine. No vitals were injured, and the mild infection she had, she worked through while we were on our little sea voyage."

"She's tough."

McKnight nodded. "Yes. She is."

"So what happened in Malibu? Nearly arrested by the FBI. No doubt you were all surfing at the time."

McKnight laughed grimly and filled his bosses in on the details of what had happened.

"Was this Tina?" he finished.

Silvia answered, "I don't think so. She says it wasn't, and I believe her."

After meeting with McKnight, she called Ching Tong into her office. Harlan was still there from the previous meeting.

"Find out anything useful?" Silvia Lewis asked. Ching Tong waggled his head from side to side.

"Yes. The code was distributed on the back of a widget upgrade through the main browser's routine update."

Harlan had spent several hours in discussion with Jess about this, and he had agreed with her theory on how the code had been disseminated.

"Which widget?" Silvia asked Ching.

"One from Realizmm."

"Never heard of Realizmm. Is that a company?"

"Yes. I hadn't heard of them either," Ching admitted. "They have a half dozen widgets, and the one that Mike chose was a keyboard interpreter."

"What does that do?" Silvia also had a software background.

"It doesn't matter. Someone needs to get into Realizmm and remove the delete code from their widget. They'll need Mike Young's help, but I guess the CIA will attend to that."

"Perhaps. What else did you find out?"

"Lots of technical stuff. And a few coding tricks. It was worth the time I spent with him."

"What sort of man is he?"

"He's a nerd. He wrote some killer code and thought he was God. Perhaps he is. But all he wanted was money, and the thought of the Chinese causing the level of destruction they had threatened really freaked him out."

Ching Tong paused.

"Having his friend tortured in front of him to make him run the code made him realize how shitty the world is, and he was disgusted that his code would be used the way it was going to be."

Ching took a sip of water before continuing.

"I actually like him. He is an honest crook. Hell, I guess I am, too."

Silvia looked her lead hacker straight in the eyes and asked, "Will he run the code for the CIA against American enemies?"

"I'm not sure. They might bribe him, but now that he's thought about the possible outcome, he might refuse."

Early that evening, at an apartment fifteen miles away, Michael McKnight knocked on the door.

"It's open. Come on in," a voice called.

He was carrying flowers and looked around the dwelling as he entered, taking in the modern touches and the stylish decor.

"I'm in here. In the bedroom."

He entered and saw Donna sitting up in bed with her hands under the covers.

"Oh, it's you." She withdrew her hands and Michael saw she was holding a Glock. She slid the safety back on and placed the gun on her side table.

"How are you feeling?" he asked.

"Better every day. And the most important thing: I'm back to blonde again."

She pointed to her hair, which had been reverted to its original color.

She noticed the flowers and said, "Nice thought. Thanks, Michael."

Michael knew the wound and her closeness to death had impacted her. She was strong and ruthless, but he feared she might decide against rolling the dice again.

"Are you coming back to Purple Frog?"

"Ha. A stupid little nine mill slug is not going to rid you of me that easily."

Chapter Thirty-Two

The FBI agents took Mike to a safe house in Arlington, Virginia and guarded him well while he had a take-in pizza and a few cold beers. He was apprehensive about what would happen next, but so far he had been treated well, although they kept a serious tone in their conversations and lacked any sense of humor.

He had liked the mysterious team who had rescued him in China and brought him to the United States. While on their week's trip from China, he had spent time with each of the team members, and since they were not techies, the conversations had not been about technical subjects. At first, he'd found this difficult, but he had softened and they'd all talked about their upbringings, some of their missions (in broad strokes), and their beliefs. He'd found himself opening up and describing his difficult home life growing up. He'd told them about his aspirations when he'd developed the delete code. McKnight had brought him up to date on Ayling's fate, and Mike had described the interchange he'd had with the First Bank of Cyprus and with Ayling. He'd wondered aloud how Bob, the janitor, had been facing the changes in Ayling Industries with the owner now deceased.

He missed the McKnight's team already.

The Chinese hacker he'd met in Malibu had said he was part of the same organization, and had been fantastic. Cate had been a good programmer, but not in the league of the Chinese guy. They had quickly developed what Mike took to be a mutual respect, and Mike had felt comfortable sharing his secrets with the short, somewhat overweight Asian.

The following day, the agents took him out to a vehicle and drove him to the CIA headquarters in Langley. They handed him over to another group of officers, who escorted him to a large, windowless room with a main table, on which were a number of large monitors and cables. A CIA IT specialist greeted him.

"Hi. I'm Buzz. I'm here to help you set up."

"Set up?"

"Yes. Your delete code laptop. This is the same spec of equipment you asked for on the West Coast."

"So, the CIA wants access to the control dashboard?"

"Of course. You're a major celebrity here at Langley. Most people with clearance know about the code and how we can use it to zap the Chinese."

Mike had known this was the likely goal of this intelligence organization, but he had hoped they would not go down this path. In his days back in Bradford, he had recognized the weaponization aspects of the code, but had thought only of using it for ransomware and monetary gain. His time in China had shown him the very dark side of what he had developed, and he knew the CIA would likely have a similar goal for its use. He had pushed this out of his mind, but now the IT techie had stated the facts clearly and he could no longer hide from the reality of the situation.

Later that day, with the setup complete and tested, he sat at the main table surrounded by a few programmers. Then several tall men entered the room. They looked just as Mike had imagined CIA officers would look. They were well built and handsome, and wore suits, button down shirts, and silk ties. Mike was almost surprised they did not wear dark glasses nor have earpieces for communications. *I'll call them "suits"* he thought.

The officers talked to each other, ignoring the hacker, and he was sure this was meant to intimidate him and indicate that he was not the star of the show.

He stared at his screen and reflected on his life. Until a month or so before, he had been a nerdy, naïve, and immature man in his early twenties who had never held a job for more than a few months, but had a mind which allowed him to write elegant and sophisticated code. Now the U.S. CIA wanted him to turn the dashboard over to them so they could destroy their enemies.

One of the suits, who appeared to be in charge, said, "Is it ready? Have you installed the code or dashboard or whatever you need?"

"Yes. It's ready to log in."

"Do it."

"Do it, *please*?"

"All right, smartass. Do it *please*."

Mike keyed in a few commands and a security screen appeared. He entered a password and then followed a series of security protocols before arriving at the dashboard.

"Done," he said.

The lead suit leaned over and looked at the screen, "I have a simple question, Young. Can we use your code to destroy all the military computers in China?"

Mike had not expected the Realizmm widget to have been incorporated into Chinese browsers, but

Dang Huan had shown him that it had been. The widget upgrade, including the delete code, had been stolen, along with many other pieces of intellectual property, and the Chinese browsers had implemented them illegally.

"Yes. That is possible."

"We've got the bastards!" The suit was ecstatic, and his colleagues reflected his enthusiasm. The programmers stood silent.

Young wondered if they would next instruct him to launch an attack on China, or whether it was just to be used as a negotiating point, or perhaps a threat.

He asked them, "Why would you want to do that?"

"They're the enemy. Destroying them is what we are supposed to do. That's our job."

A woman entered the room and the agents turned to her.

One of the programmers spoke for the first time. "Hi, Tina. You've got to hear this. We can use this hacker's code to destroy China."

"That decision is above your pay grade, Bill."

The suit in charge said, "This is a great breakthrough. This little bastard and his code is going to get us all promotions. China is toast."

"That's my decision, Chuck. Don't get too excited."

Young could see that the suits harbored resentment towards the short woman, and he wondered if it was a sexist attitude or whether the director was resented for other reasons.

She ignored her subordinates and turned to face him.

"Michael Young? I'm Tina Graham and I'm pleased to meet you at last. How are you doing? You had a rough time."

This was the first time anyone in the CIA had asked about his wellbeing and he grinned.

In the past few weeks, he had endured a lot with everyone treating him badly, until the mystery team who rescued him and their Chinese hacker had offered a kinder approach. Now he was back with a group of men treating him badly.

That was, until Tina Graham joined the meeting and he found her softer attitude a welcome relief.

The CIA director and Mike chatted about various matters unrelated to the code for a few minutes while the men around showed obvious impatience. The senior suit apparently decided that it was time to take charge.

"Tina, we're wasting time. Let's see what this little fucker can do for us."

Tina Graham snarled at the agent and then said quietly, "Mike, can you show us what your code can do?"

Mike had made up his mind. He had been thinking about a course of action from the time the FBI had picked him up in Malibu and through the flight to Washington. He knew what he had to do, but he sat still for a minute in front of his screen, thinking of the impact of his next action.

The suit snapped, "Okay, Young, show us how this works. There are three computers on a separate network and they are over there on that table. Zap 'em."

Mike's system had timed out, so he needed to log in again. He flexed his fingers, then entered a string of security protocols which allowed him to access the delete code's dashboard.

"It all works from here. I key in search parameters or IP addresses and individual computer identifiers, and the software isolates the target systems. Then I hit the Delete button and that sends a command to each target computer, and as you've just said, it zaps them."

"Show us."

Tina stood still, watching what her intuition had told her would happen next.

Mike smiled and the suits missed seeing a look of determination appear on his face. He keyed in an IP address and computer identification and paused. "You're sure of this?"

"Yes, Young. Get on with it," the head suit snarled.

He clicked his mouse on the Delete button.

His screen went blank.

"What the hell just happened?" the suit asked.

"I guess I keyed in the wrong identifier. Looks like I destroyed my computer and its dashboard and the backup. The delete code still resides on two billion computers, but it can't be activated now except by accident or by meddling."

"Get it back. Restore it or whatever."

"Not possible. It's gone."

"You little bastard." The lead suit was furious. Tina nodded with a small smile, acknowledging the courage the hacker had finally shown.

It was 3 a.m. and Jason heard Sarah's cries of pain. He called Doctor Stephens who injected some additional pain killer to her frail body and then turned to Jason.

"It won't be long. Probably in the next hour."

"I'll get the girls."

A short time later, he stood by the bed with his two daughters, Elsie and Doris. He held Sarah's hand and she opened her eyes smiled at him and then sank into sleep. Or was it sleep? Stephens stepped forward and checked for vital signs. He frowned and then turned to the others in the room and shook his head.

Jason's daughters' husbands flew down for the ceremony.

The men arrived at the house late at night, and after a short supper, retired to their bedrooms. Jason stayed up and walked into the bar. Doris was standing there. Her eyes showed that she had been crying, but she quickly wiped them and faked a smile.

"What can I get you, Mr. Overly?"

"Doris, I thought we were over that. Call me Jason. Please."

He faked a smile, but the corners of his mouth then drooped and his head dropped.

"Doris, what am I going to do? The love of my life is gone." He cried and held his head in his hands.

Doris came from behind the bar and hugged him. "Jason, she's gone to God now." She was also now freely crying, and then Jason's daughters entered the bar area.

"Hubbies are in bed, dad," Olivia said. "Let's all get smashed and mourn Mom."

Doris dabbed at her eyes and said, "I'll leave you, then."

Olivia placed a hand on her arm. "No, Doris. You're part of this family. Please stay."

"Thank you."

Jason walked around the bar and said, "My turn here. What will everyone have?"

As Jason poured drinks, August started the conversation they all wanted. "Do you remember that crazy time when Mom..."

The next morning, Olivia and August, their husbands, and Elsie met Jason for breakfast. He addressed them.

"Your mom and I discussed what she wanted us to do." A tear rolled down his face and he continued. "She asked to be cremated and for her ashes to be scattered on the water out beyond the reef. She was insistent that she did not want a big deal made of the cremation, and she only wanted family members out on the boat. That obviously includes you, Doris. Darnell will skipper.

"In a few weeks, I'll fly back to our home in California and we'll have an upbeat memorial service. Sarah was adamant about that, too. No grief. Just great memories from what she described as a wonderful life."

Darnell drove the boat out through the cutting and into the waters beyond the reef.

"Here?" he asked Jason.

"A little further out. Where we can have a clear view of the house."

Darnell put the throttle into drive and moved the boat to where Jason indicated. Jason nodded and Darnell kept the boat steady.

Doris brought up the simple urn in which Sarah's ashes resided and handed it to Jason. He walked to the edge of the boat and looked at the urn. "Darling, I shall always love you." Then, almost as an afterthought, he turned to Doris. "Doris, I am not a praying man, but would you please say a prayer for Sarah?"

Doris stepped forward and voiced the words as Olivia and August hugged their dad. When she finished, Jason uncapped the urn and was about to pour out the ashes when a school of young dolphins rose from the sea and surrounded the boat. They played with one another as if they wanted to make a show, then disappeared into the depths. Jason scattered the ashes, and as they made their way back to shore, the school of dolphins reappeared and kept pace with the boat all the way into Sugar Bay.

Chapter Thirty-Three

Tina was still processing the stunt Mike Young had pulled. If he was to be believed—and there seemed no reason not to believe him—the power of the delete code was gone. Although the code was still present on most of the computers worldwide, without a mechanism to activate it, the threat had been removed. As, too, was the potential opportunity.

Her senior staff had been furious and had been on the point of physically assaulting the programmer, but Tina had stopped them.

She called the president and met with him in the Oval Office to inform him of what had happened. He, too, was angry. Coming from a situation where the malware had become his worst nightmare, he had quickly embraced the idea that he now had control of the weapon and would be able to threaten China and the other enemies of the United States, just as Yang had threatened him. Now the stage was neutral again, and after the huge win having the hacker and his code had given him, he now faced a situation where the win had turned into a draw.

Tina offered a consolation prize. "Mr. President, no one needs to know that we have lost the code. We can still use it as a threat. China knows how powerful it is, or was, and we could dangle it as a sword over their heads."

The president of the most powerful nation on earth sat down in his chair behind the Resolute desk. "Let me think about that. Perhaps we could get away with it once, but after that..."

He shook his head.

"What a fucking lost opportunity. Can't you get this Brit to rewrite the dashboard or whatever it is?"

"We've tried already, but he is adamant that he cannot, or will not, do that."

"Try again."

"We can try, but he seems to have made up his mind."

"Then get him to change his mind. Offer him money. Threaten him. Do what you have to do."

"I'll try, Mr. President."

"Don't try, Director. Do it." The president saw a glimmer of hope in resurrecting the situation.

Returning from the White House, Tina Graham's driver let her out in the underground carpark at Langley and she took the elevator to the top floor, where her office was located. Her personal assistant was waiting. "How did it go, Ms. Graham?"

"He is no longer my greatest admirer." Tina entered her office, threw her bag onto a chair, and sat at her desk. Her PA had sent her a list of issues and she perused these to ensure that none were urgent, then dialed the number for Well-wisher."

"Hi, Well-wisher," she said when the call was answered.

"What's up?" Silvia barked, and she knew the CIA director could tell she was still mad as hell with her.

"I shouldn't be telling you any of this," Tina said, "but I need to vent, and I can't do it with anyone at the agency."

Silvia was sarcastic. "Oh. I guess that's what friends are for. Okay, Tina. Do it. Vent!"

"Our little hacker friend did a delete on his own system and the dashboard for activating the code is now gone. The strategic advantage that it gave us has been eliminated."

"Was it accidental?"

"No. Deliberate. He saw the potential and decided that no person or nation should have it."

"I can see his point."

"The president and my senior staff are all furious."

"That's a blow, Tina." Silvia smiled. "Can't you persuade him to build another dashboard? If he could do it the first time, he could no doubt do it again."

"People in my organization are attempting that, but our scared little programmer seems to have grown an extra set of balls. He'll be a tough nut to crack. He told one of my senior agents to, and I quote, 'Go fuck yourself, asshole.' "

"It sounds like you are being pressured to use threats, or even physical persuasion?"

"The president has been clear—break Mike Young any way I can."

"I had a feeling we should have kept him away from you."

"Come on. You'd have done the same if you had him. You'd use him as leverage to foster your world peace goals."

Silvia reflected on this before Tina continued.

"Your influence on world policy would have been enormous."

"It did pass through my mind."

Silvia knew the power Purple Frog would have had if Mike had stayed in their organization, but having that type and magnitude of power might be just too much.

"Tina, I think you're secretly happy that Mike did what he did."

Tina sighed.

"We'll see what the president instructs me to do next. If it were up to me, I would declare victory and move back to the conventional fights and skirmishes that we've had for decades."

While Tina Graham was meeting with the president, Mike Young sat in the conference room with the suits who were still fuming.

The senior suit paced up and down until a call came in to his smartphone.

He picked up, "Yes, Director?"

He listened for a minute and then hung up.

"Okay, you little shit, we're taking you back to the safe house."

Young asked, "With the code gone, what are you going to do with me now?"

"We'll stand over you until you re-write it."

The hacker laughed "Not going to happen."

"We'll see."

The senior suit turned to one of his men and ordered, "Bring the cars around to the front."

The suit frowned, "Shouldn't we take him out through the underground carpark?"

"Why bother. We have a detail of five officers to protect him. What could go wrong?"

The motorcade drew up to the front entrance of the CIA and the hacker was bundled out of the building towards the central vehicle.

The sound of gunfire punctuated the early evening air, and a hail of bullets tore into the group. The senior suit was struck in the throat by one of them. His people returned the fire that was coming from a heavily armed group hidden behind cars in the visitor parking lot.

Mike Young ducked for cover. *Why the hell didn't I just get a programming job at the local council in Bradford?* he thought.

Silvia heard some background noise on her call with Tina, and for an instant wondered if the CIA director was trying to trace her location.

Then Tina interrupted and said, "Wait a minute. I have an urgent message."

Silvia listened to Tina's voice in the background as she dealt with the emergency. She picked up a few snippets of the conversation.

"He's been what? How the hell could that have happened?"

She came back on the line with Silvia.

"I have a crisis. I'll call you back."

Silvia's mind went into overdrive. What had the fragments of Tina's offline conversation meant?

Silvia made coffee and sipped it while she waited for Tina to call back. It was an hour before the CIA director placed that call.

"When we were speaking an hour ago, you may have heard some of what was going on in that emergency," Tina said.

"It didn't sound good."

"It's not." Tina exhaled. "A team was escorting Young back to his safe house. We had five officers guarding him. Then a group of armed men appeared out of nowhere and engaged them. The attackers had heavy duty assault weapons and grenades."

"What happened?"

"One of my men was killed and two were injured, but we fought well and shot all six of the attackers. They all perished."

"Who were the attackers?"

"They were Asian. My guess would be Chinese."

"And Young?"

"They shot him."

"Oh, God. Is he all right?"

"No; he's dead. He was their target. It's obvious that Yang decided to level the playing field."

Silvia paused to take a sip of coffee and pulled a face as she realized it was cold.

"I guess both the threat and the potential for the delete code has ended. China doesn't have it. We don't have it. No one has it."

Silvia waited for Tina to complete her narrative, guessing what would come next.

"Don't ever tell the president or any of my staff, but I personally count that as a win. A win for the world."

"We're in synch on that."

They talked for a few minutes more as Silvia learned the details of the incident, then she terminated the call. She called Harlan and briefed him on what Tina had told her.

At the other end of the Purple Frog offices, Ching Tong was thinking about his first date with Ginny, which would take place in just a few hours. The Spanish profiler had changed her mind about the Chinese hacker and had agreed to meet him for a drink and, perhaps, dinner. He knew she probably saw him as an egotistical elitist, and he certainly did not look like Jackie Chan, but he reasoned that Ginny was also feeling the isolation and remoteness that their job brought with it. Perhaps just a drink and a laugh. Or perhaps something more.

He moved on from his flight of fancy and pulled up an access screen on his computer. He followed a complex login protocol, which took significant concentration, and then the screen hesitated for a second or so. A dashboard appeared with a large button at the bottom of the screen labeled "Delete." Ching smiled at the copy of Mike's dashboard, which he had made when he and the hacker had worked together at the house in Malibu, before Young had been transferred to the CIA.

This might be useful, one day, he thought, and he saved the file.

End of Book Seven

Coming Soon

Brisa's Grief

Book 8 in the Purple Frog Series

A DEA team raids the headquarters of a South American drug cartel, but things don't go as planned and the daughter of the cartel chief seeks revenge on the United States. She develops a new narcotic which she plans to release, killing several million Americans.

With political tensions running high, the U.S. governmental agencies are unable to act, and the task of preventing the disaster falls to Purple Frog.

Coming later in 2022 and early 2023

Assault and Batteries

Book 9

One of the richest men in the world, November Swan, decides to enhance his wealth further by cornering a new technology for electric vehicle batteries. He uses every gambit to secure the technology, fight off his competitors, and gain government approvals. His tactics extend beyond normal as he resorts to immoral and illegal actions to accomplish his goals.

His Final Bow

Book 10

This is the final book in the Purple Frog series, and follows the path of a member of Purple Frog who faces death and puts in place a final ploy to drive peace across the planet.

About the Author:

Harry Bunn has traveled to over fifty countries worldwide, and has resided in Sydney, Australia; London, England; and Princeton, NJ. He founded an international marketing consulting firm focused on the technology sector, managed it for thirty years, and is now retired in St. Croix in the U.S. Virgin Islands, where he lives with his wife, Jackie. They have two sons, James and Nicholas. Harry has taken up writing since his retirement, with a variety of themes, but his focus has been on a series of thrillers--Purple Frog.

Contact him at harrybunnauthor@gmail.com, or check out his website for news on new books, and get access to a range of "freebies," including short stories, his blog, and a few mystery items.

https://www.lifemadesimple.store/publishing.

Other Purple Frog Books

Purple Frog (Book 1)

Jason Overly, a technology billionaire, funds a daring rogue operation devoted to world peace. This international team employs unorthodox methods, including hacking, blackmail, extortion, and occasionally, murder. The group has been given the name Purple Frog after a little-known frog that spends most of its time underground, out of sight, emerging only for two weeks each year. Keeping below the radar is key to Purple Frog's success, but a plot to assassinate the new president of the European Union calls for more direct action and the risk of discovery.

MetalWorks (Book 2)

Frederik Verwoerd is successful and rich, but wants more. His desire is to become a major player on the world stage, and he decides that his South African armament company, MetalWorks, will develop a new weapon of mass destruction, which he will sell to the highest bidder. The weapon is neither nuclear, chemical, nor biological, but can destroy an army of five thousand tanks in the field, or even a major city. To demonstrate its power, he targets a well-protected symbol of the United States and will telecast its destruction live.

It falls to Purple Frog, a private and clandestine organization, to stop him, but to do so, Purple Frog must reveal its existence to the CIA. However, it is already facing a threat from the Russian president, who wants to locate and punish the organization.

Brotherhood of the Skull (Book 3)

Outside Washington, DC, one million armed white supremacists have assembled to march on the capital and seize power. They are led by Gideon Page, a charismatic but ruthless white supremacist, and Jonathan Greer, a televangelist. They have a symbol for their insurrection: an ancient skull previously owned by Adolf Hitler. A rogue U.S. senator, Jeffrey Kendall, has teamed up with them and expects to become the new president of the United States after the Brotherhood of the Skull overthrows the present elected government.

Law enforcement is hamstrung by legalities and political correctness, but the clandestine Purple Frog organization has no such limitations and moves to thwart this attack on American democracy.

Citadel of Yakutsk (Book 4)

"The Citadel is the real threat." The dying words of the CIA Chief of Station in Moscow are cryptic, but no one knows what his message means. Yakutsk is a remote city in Siberia. It boasts the coldest weather of any city on the planet, and is home to a clandestine facility in subterranean caves deep beneath the conurbation. This secret metropolis is the headquarters of Alexi Rackov, a Russian general who has developed a plan to expand Russian territory by invading eight countries, and bringing eighty-eight million European citizens under Russian hegemony. While there are rumors about such a site, these only identify its name: the Citadel. Its location and mission are known only to Rackov and Dobry Petrovski, the Russian president.

In the United States, Purple Frog is a secret organization established by Jason Overly, a tech billionaire, with the mission to foster world peace. Though Purple Frog parallels the CIA and MI6, it operates outside the rules and political correctness of these intelligence organizations. It will face its greatest challenge as its small team strives to prevent the annexation of these Eastern European countries.

Flag Eight (Book 5)

A new president in Venezuela, Mateo Videgain, is facing a multitude of problems, including a collapsed economy. He regards the United States as a major reason for this and his main enemy, deciding on a bold plan to consolidate his place in history.

Just 520 miles to the north is the U.S. territory of St. Croix, and Videgain decides to invade and occupy the island.

All hell breaks loose as, with help from Russia, his helicopters, warships, and troops attack. When the locals fight back against his vastly superior forces, the battle is short and the Venezuelans take control.

Few countries have been ruled by seven different nations, but over the five hundred and twenty-eight years since St. Croix's discovery by Christopher Columbus, it has been a territory of Spain, France, the Netherlands, England, the Knights of Malta, Denmark, and most recently, the U.S. In total, seven flags have flown over the island. The Venezuelan president raises his flag over the territory--*flag eight*.

He has not, however, factored in that Jason Overly, who has a home on the island, is also the head of a clandestine intelligence operation called Purple Frog, which will do whatever is necessary to stop the plans of the Venezuelan president.

To Venice with Love (Book 6)

Alan Harlan and his new wife, Jess, embark on their honeymoon to a Greek island, but they encounter an old enemy and a Saudi prince who have deployed a bioweapon on an ecologically advanced super yacht. Alan and Jess find themselves on the vessel's maiden voyage from Athens to Venice, discover the plot, and need to identify which of the passengers or crew will be responsible for triggering the device on their arrival in Venice.

Alan is head of operations for Purple Frog, a clandestine organization mirroring the CIA and MI6, but with fewer constraints. He brings many of Purple Frog's resources into play as they battle the forces striving to destroy this romantic Italian city's population, together with one million visiting tourists.

Made in the USA
Columbia, SC
09 August 2023